A BASEBALL GREAT NOVEL

HARPER

An Imprint of HarperCollins*Publishers*

ST OF THE ST

A BASEBALL GREAT NOVEL

TIM GREEN

ALSO BY TIM GREEN

BASEBALL GREAT NOVELS

Baseball Great
Rivals

FOOTBALL GENIUS NOVELS

Football Genius
Football Hero
Football Champ
The Big Time

Best of the Best: A Baseball Great Novel

www.harpercollinschildrens.com

Library of Congress Cataloging-in-Publication Data

Green, Tim.

Best of the best: a baseball great novel / by Tim Green. — 1st ed.

p. cm.

Summary: Determined to play in the Little League World Series, twelve-year-old Josh struggles to concentrate on his game and be the team's leader while also trying to cope with his parents' impending divorce.

ISBN 978-0-06-168622-1 (trade bdg.) — ISBN 978-0-06-168623-8 (lib. bdg.)

[1. Baseball—Fiction. 2. Divorce—Fiction.] I. Title.

PZ7.G826357Be 2011 2010022976

[Fic]—dc22 CIP

AC

Typography by Joel Tippie

11 12 13 14 15 CG/RRDH 10 9 8 7 6 5 4 3 2 1

❖

First Edition

For Illyssa, because you really are the best of the best

CHAPTER ONE

A SILENT STORM OF moths, June bugs, and mosquitoes swarmed the powerful light high above Josh and his father. It was a hot, dark night. Heat radiated up from the blacktop surface of the batting cage, warming the bottoms of Josh's sneakers. The rest of the team had already gone home, but not Josh. Extra work was something he hungered for, especially under his father's trained eye.

His father pointed to the knob on the pitching machine that controlled its speed and said, "I think you're ready for ninety."

Josh swallowed. Ninety miles an hour was a fastball you might see in college or even the pros, and even though he stood nearly six feet tall, he was still just twelve. He stepped back and tilted the brim of his batting helmet with a thumb.

"That scare you?" his father asked. "It's okay if it does. It should."

"A little," Josh said. "'Cause I won't see anything like it for five or six years."

"Oh, it might be a bit sooner than that," his father said. "I wouldn't do it if I didn't think you could handle it."

"Could you hit a ninety-mile-an-hour ball when you were twelve?" Josh asked.

"Me?" his father said, his eyebrows disappearing up under the blue shadow cast by the brim of his hat. "No. I was your size when I was twelve, but I didn't have your skills. That's why we do this. I want to make sure you develop everything you've got. I want you to go further than me."

"You were a first-round pick," Josh said.

His father waved an impatient hand and said, "That doesn't mean anything. It's about the majors, and I never made it. Relax, I'm okay with it. I'm beginning to think I was cut out for coaching anyway. You, though, you can make it all the way."

"You really think so?" Josh asked, not for the first time.

"I know so," his father said. "Everyone who sees you knows you've got it. Now we have to bring it along. That's why I want you to try this. Think about it: if you can hit a pitch going ninety, there isn't a pitcher you'll see for the rest of the year whose fastest ball won't look like it's coming at you in slow motion."

Josh nodded and tightened his grip and stepped up to the plate. When the first yellow rubber batting cage ball came at him, Josh didn't even swing. He had grown used to seeing the pitch leave the machine—or a pitcher's hand—and being able to read the spin of the ball. This was something else. It was almost like he had blinked, even though he knew he hadn't.

His father chuckled. "It's okay. You'll get used to it. Watch a few first."

Two balls later, Josh clenched his teeth and readied his bat. *Plunk* went the machine, and the pitch came like a bullet. Josh swung, and nicked it.

"That's it," his father said.

Josh got a decent piece of the next two.

"Almost there, Josh," his father said with real excitement ready to burst from his throat.

Josh felt the thrill of his father's praise and the next ball he hammered, driving it past the pitching machine and into the back of the net.

"Excellent!" his father crowed.

Josh heard a delicate clapping and turned to see Jaden—one of his two best friends—sitting atop her ten-speed bike, balancing against the outside of the cage with one toe jammed into the space between two fence links. Josh gave her a smile and kept at it. It wasn't long before Josh was banging them steadily. When the bin of balls stood empty, Josh's father, a mountain of a man, crossed the space between them and hugged Josh tight.

"That's my boy," his father said, and Josh beamed. "All right, let me see ten bunt steps."

"Dad," Josh said with a groan, "I just hit a ninety-mile-an-hour fastball."

"Never forget your basics," his father said, extending the bat Josh had leaned against the fence. "You never know when you'll have to bunt. You've got to stay sharp, even with the small stuff."

"Can you at least pitch some balls at me?"

"Basics," his father said. "Footwork is the key."

Josh could only nod. He took the bat, stepped up to the plate, and executed the step he'd take across the plate if he were to bunt.

"Loosen your shoulders just a bit. You've got to absorb the energy of the ball. That's it."

Finally Josh finished.

"Good," his father said, grinning. "Now let's go get an ice cream. Jaden? How about you?"

"Thanks, Mr. LeBlanc," Jaden said, wiping her brow with the back of one hand.

Josh stuffed his equipment into his bat bag and shouldered it before following his father out of the cage, where he froze in his tracks. Walking toward them from the parking lot was a woman who was pretty enough to be on TV. She had shoulder-length glossy dark hair and pale blue eyes that sparkled at Josh's father.

"Hello," she said, holding out a hand that Josh's father took before kissing her cheek.

Josh's stomach clenched with the fear of a nightmare coming true.

The woman glanced at him and said, "This must be your son, Josh."

Josh's father cleared his throat and said, "It is."

"So nice to finally meet you," the woman said, extending a hand that Josh reluctantly shook before watching the woman do the same thing to Jaden.

"Josh," his dad said, "this is Diane. She's the one who's been showing me all the new houses."

"Oh," Josh said, and he knew the hatred in his eyes must be burning like the flame from a welding torch.

"And there's something that just came on the market you've got to see," Diane said. "I think it'll move right away, and I want you to see it before anyone else."

"It's nine-thirty," Josh's dad said.

"I've got friends in high places," Diane said with a wave of her hand. "Come on, you can't say no."

"To you?" Josh's dad had a silly grin. "No, I guess I can't. Josh? You okay walking home with Jaden?"

Josh wanted to protest, but Jaden spoke up first and said, "We're fine, Mr. LeBlanc. It's such a nice night."

Josh watched his father go before he turned to Jaden with a scowl.

"What?" she said. "You didn't want him to go with her? She seemed nice. What's wrong?"

Josh unclenched his teeth and said, "Everything."

CHAPTER TWO

A THREE-FOOT TROPHY STOOD on the floor in the corner of Josh's tiny bedroom, mocking him. All his life Josh heard coaches say that winning was everything, or the only thing, but right now those words sounded foolish. Because his ceiling was tucked up into the eaves of the old house's roof, there hadn't been headroom for the shiny metal prize on his dresser. Josh slipped out of bed, disgusted at the memory of the night before when Diane showed up and things went downhill. He wadded up an old pair of underwear and pitched it at the trophy so that it hung from its golden peak, completely covering the figure of a batter. Josh turned away and began to dress, his mind on his parents, their argument when his father finally got home from house hunting, and how he'd heard the word *divorce*.

Josh knew none of it would have happened without the five-year coaching contract his father had signed with Nike. He knew his father wouldn't have gone to look at new homes in the suburbs without the guaranteed money that came with the Nike deal. Without the contract, his father wouldn't have met the Realtor named Diane Cross with her white Audi convertible and her voice like a purring cat. Josh had heard his mom call Diane "a shameless tramp" during one of their arguments. Then he heard his father reply that Diane was a nice person and that men were allowed to have women as friends. That made sense to Josh because Jaden Neidermeyer was also a girl.

But even Josh knew the difference between two seventh graders and an ex-professional baseball player riding around town in a convertible with a pretty woman who was already divorced herself. Josh felt guilty because he had been largely responsible for the Nike deal. The deal—which sponsored the Titans U12 team—had come from beating a Los Angeles team coached by a very famous former baseball player in the Hall of Fame National Championship game. Without Josh's batting and defense at shortstop, the Titans wouldn't have stood a chance.

He brushed his teeth and spit in the sink.

When Josh tiptoed down the stairs, his heart sank even further. His father was stretched out on the couch, snoring through his open mouth. Josh tried to sneak across the room without waking him, but just as Josh stepped into the kitchen, he heard his father clear his throat. Josh turned. His father sat up, stroking the scruff on his chin. An enormous man with long limbs, Josh's father had a voice like distant thunder.

"Josh," he said, rising so that the blanket fell from him and he stood in boxers and a T-shirt, his legs hairy and thick as tree trunks. "Where you going?"

"I tried to be quiet," Josh said. "I've got three lawns to cut before batting practice."

"That's okay," his father said. "I wanted to talk to you."

The tone of his father's voice made Josh afraid to ask what it was he wanted to talk about, so Josh only said, "I heard you talking when you came home last night, Dad. I wasn't listening, but I heard you from my room, so I know what this is about."

His father sighed and hung his head, scratching the back of his neck before he looked up at Josh with puffy red eyes.

"Josh," he said, "sometimes opportunities pop up like—I don't know, like targets in a shooting gallery. If you want to win the prize, you've got to take your shots."

Josh shook his head.

"Here," his father said, guiding him into the kitchen and pulling out a chair so Josh could sit down. "You sit. I'll get you some cereal. I know this is going to be hard for you to understand, but I've been thinking about it a lot, Josh, and I want you to listen with an open mind. Can you do that?"

Josh bit his lower lip and nodded his head.

"I'll try."

CHAPTER THREE

JOSH'S FATHER TOOK A box of Cheerios from the cupboard and gathered up a bowl, a spoon, and a carton of milk from the fridge. He set them before Josh, then turned on the coffeemaker before sitting down across from him at the small round table tucked into the corner of the kitchen. A thick beam of early morning summer sun fell into the room through the window over the sink. Josh could see the lines of worry and age carved into his father's face, lines he didn't remember from before.

"Believe me," his father said, "the easiest thing for me would be to keep things exactly as they are, but I'm thinking of you, Josh."

"I want us all to be together, Dad," Josh said, blurting out the words. "I want that more than anything."

His father sighed again and said, "I know. That's

what we all want, but things change. Here, get going on your cereal and just listen. The final decision will be yours, but I want you to hear both sides of the story."

Josh poured cereal into the bowl and spilled the milk in his confusion over his father's words about the final decision being his. His father got a cloth and poured himself a cup of coffee before returning. Josh took the cloth and mopped up the spill with trembling hands. The worst part for Josh would be choosing who to live with, his mother or his father. He knew that was the question on his father's lips. To keep from crying, Josh shoveled in a mouthful of cereal and began to work his jaw.

"A lot of famous players used this as a stepping-stone to do great things in the majors," Josh's father said. "I mean, Derek Bell and Gary Sheffield, just off the top of my head. I think it's the right thing for you, too, Josh. Even though it means leaving the Titans for the next couple of months."

Josh's mouth fell open and some soggy Cheerios dribbled down his chin before plopping onto the table.

"Josh?" his father said. "You okay?"

"Titans?" Josh said. "I'm leaving the Titans? What are you talking about? I thought you meant you and Mom. That change."

Josh's father's face flushed and he looked down. "No, that's not what I'm talking about. That's another discussion. You said you heard me talking. I thought you meant you heard me on the phone with Coach Quatropanni."

"Coach Q?" Josh wiped his chin. "My Little League coach? Dad, what are you talking about?"

Even though Josh spent countless hours practicing and playing for the Titans, his father had insisted that he also play for a Little League team in his spare moments. Josh convinced Benji to do it with him, and they both played for Coach Quatropanni and his Delmonico Insurance Little League team whenever they didn't have to play or practice with the Titans travel team. With Josh's exceptional talent, Coach Q had been happy to have them on the team, even though Josh and Benji never made a practice and missed many of the games.

At the time Josh first heard the idea of playing Little League, he thought his dad was crazy. But his dad had been a first-round draft choice out of high school by the Mets and spent twelve years around the minor leagues before retiring. His dad knew the world of baseball as well as anyone, so Josh had agreed, even though he felt funny just showing up to the games.

"Well, believe it or not, you actually made it to half the regular season games with Delmonico's," Josh's father said, "and that qualifies you to play on the league's all-star team. They gave Coach Q the Lyncourt All-Stars this year, and they've already won the local round of playoffs while we were in Cooperstown. I guess a couple kids had to drop out, though, so . . . ”

“Dad,” Josh said, “no offense, but we just won the Hall of Fame National Championship. I was on HBO with Bob Costas. Why would I care about the Lyncourt Little League All-Stars?”

His dad held up a hand and said, “I know. We won a national championship, and it was great, and we've got this awesome Nike deal and—believe me—we've got a lot left to accomplish with the Titans. But Coach Q has his sights set on playing in the Little League World Series. It's a long shot, but, you know, Coach Q says that the Lyncourt all-star team this year is the best group he's ever seen. They've got those Fries brothers and that kid Fedchenko, who can really sling it. I'm thinking about recruiting all three of them for the Titans. And Josh? With your bat, honestly? Anything's possible. They see that, and I see something that you'll never forget. Selfishly, do I want you to miss the next two months of tournaments with the Titans? Of course not. But for you, Son, this is a once-in-a-lifetime chance. You'll never get it again. Hey, who knows? You guys might not make it through the districts in Albany next week, then everything will be back to normal.

“But,” his dad said, his brown eyes losing their focus as he peered past Josh and blinked into the glare of the kitchen window, “if you do make it? Josh, you'll be playing against teams from all over the *world*, the best of the best.

"But I said the decision is yours, and I meant it. What do you think?"

CHAPTER FOUR

JOSH'S HEAD SPUN. PART of him felt giddy that the news had nothing to do with his parents splitting up, but he reminded himself that his father said that was another discussion. The breakup was still out there, creeping around like a serial killer in the bushes, looking for a way in.

"Can Benji do it with me?" Josh asked, the idea coming to him from thin air. Benji Lido, Josh's other best friend, was a heavyset seventh grader with a sense of humor as big as his appetite.

Josh's dad raised his eyebrows. "I can't say. They didn't ask, but I know they want you pretty bad. They might do it."

"I'm in," Josh said, breaking out into a grin.

"Even if Benji can't?" his father asked.

"I don't know," Josh said. "Can I think about it?"

His father smiled and pointed to the cereal. "Sure. I'll call Coach Q. We can meet with him after batting practice and see about Benji. Eat up. I don't want to keep you from your work."

Josh gobbled down the rest of his cereal and rinsed the bowl. His mom shuffled in, the bottoms of her slippers scratching the linoleum floor. Josh's little sister, Laurel, rested on his mom's hip, rubbing the sleep from her eyes.

"Good morning, Josh," his mom said, pointedly ignoring Josh's father.

"Hi, Mom," Josh said, his heart aching at the sight of his mom's sad face. "I'm going to cut Mrs. Cunningham's lawn, then the Keegans' and Jacksons' before batting practice."

He kissed her cheek, then the top of his little sister's head, then his dad before scooting out the door.

From the detached garage, Josh dragged the lawn mower, pushing it down the sidewalk, up over the broken seams toward the first lawn on his list. As he walked, he texted Jaden to tell her to swing by if she had a minute. He wanted to tell her about the World Series in person. Jaden, more than even him or Benji, loved baseball and everything about it. She'd know the significance of a quest for the Little League World Series.

Josh came to a stop in front of a chain-link fence

surrounding a yard riddled with dog poop. The pale blue house belonged to a white-haired old woman who could hardly hear. Still, she paid twenty-five dollars for the job, five more than Josh's going rate. He had five lawns he cut in all, including his own, and he was able to save a good bit of money from the work. It was his mom who insisted on him working, even though his dad said he preferred Josh spend all his free time on baseball.

An evil part of him in the darkest corner of his mind thought that if his parents *did* separate, he might not have to cut lawns anymore. The better part of him squashed that thought, and so he began, stepping carefully and breathing through his mouth whenever one of the lawn mower's wheels came up with a surprise. The thick grass bled green juice that stained Josh's sneakers and filled the air, tamping down the smell of dog poop. Josh had worked up a sweat by the time he was done.

He held his hand out patiently as the smiling old woman counted out twenty-five one-dollar bills, then wiped his brow as he descended the porch. The sun peeked over the trees, promising a scorcher. Josh shaded his eyes as he wheeled the mower through the gate, and so the white Audi appeared as if by magic. Almost before the scene could register in his brain, Diane Cross popped out of her car and stood blocking his way on the sidewalk. She wore a tight black skirt and an even tighter white blouse. Around her shoulder she'd slung a big purse as red as her lips. Even though Josh stood just under six feet tall—more than half a foot over this woman, even with her high heels—she somehow made him feel small.

Trying not to sound as ruffled as he felt, Josh glared down into her sunglasses and asked, "What do you want?"

"Hello, Josh," she said, smooth and soft. "We need to talk."

CHAPTER FIVE

"I DON'T HAVE ANYTHING to say to you," Josh said, wheeling the mower up onto the grass and steering past her.

Josh got to the next driveway hearing the click of her heels on the sidewalk, coming fast. She tapped his shoulder, and he spun around.

"I know this isn't easy for you, Josh," she said, "but it happens. Sometimes people don't get it right the first time. Your father and I, well, this is it. The real thing this time."

Josh's mouth fell open.

"And I want us to be friends, Josh," she said

"Are you crazy?" Josh said, almost to himself.

A smile snaked across her lips. "Crazy for your father."

"Stop it!" Josh said. "Stop talking like that. You're

not my friend. You're . . . you're . . . "

Josh dug deep for the word he'd heard his mother use.

"You're a tramp!"

"You have no idea what you're talking about," Diane said, snapping off her sunglasses. "And if you're going to be nasty to me, you're going to get it right back, mister.

"But I'm sure we'll figure a way to get along," she said, batting her eyelids and looking innocent and beautiful, as if she'd pulled on a mask.

Josh realized this wasn't for him when he saw her eyes flicker past his shoulder. He turned and watched Jaden Neidermeyer close the gap between them on the sidewalk. Jaden was big for a girl of twelve but stood straight like she belonged there. Her hair was frizzy and dark, and she kept it pulled into a ponytail. Her skin was the color of coffee with milk, and the features on her face were delicate, almost elfish. Josh thought she was the prettiest girl in the whole school.

"Hey, Josh," Jaden said, her green cat eyes shifting with uncertainty. "You wanted to talk to me?"

"You're the girl from the batting cage," Diane said, her voice syrupy sweet.

"Jaden, remember?" Jaden said, extending a hand.

"And manners, too." Diane shifted her purse to shake hands. "Of course you're Jaden. Do you know my son, Marcus? Marcus Cross? No, well, he goes to

Bishop Grimes. He's such a great kid. Everyone likes him, but I think they have a different set of friends than the public school kids, not that there's anything wrong with public school."

This was the first Josh had heard about Diane having a son, and it only made his head swim faster.

"Josh is going to be playing some baseball with Marcus on the Lyncourt all-star team," Diane said. "In fact, that's why I stopped, to congratulate him on being part of the team. Do you like baseball?"

"I'm a Yankees fan," Jaden said, "and I covered the Titans at the Hall of Fame tournament for the *Post-Standard*."

"Covered?"

"I'm a writer," Jaden said. "For the newspaper."

"Really?"

"I want to win a Pulitzer," Jaden said. "That's one day, though."

"If you're already writing for the paper," Diane said, "you're certainly on your way, and such a pretty girl. You should go into TV. You could be on a show."

"No," Jaden said, "just writing."

"Well," Diane said, "it was a real pleasure to meet you. And Josh, thanks for our little talk. I know how much you mean to your father, and it's good to know you're the kind of boy who thinks about his happiness, too. So many kids today think only of themselves."

Diane turned and marched down the sidewalk. She

climbed into her car and pulled away with a toot and a wave.

"Wow. She's nice," Jaden said. "Do you know her son?"

Josh just looked at her.

CHAPTER SIX

"WHAT'S WRONG?" JADEN ASKED.

Josh wiped the sweat from his forehead and started pushing the mower down the sidewalk, shaking his head.

"Josh?"

Josh kept pushing until he reached a big old white house with black shutters and two gigantic trees shading the entire front lawn. He bent down to pull the motor to life. Jaden poked his shoulder.

"I'm not going away. You text me that you've got some news, then you start acting like a zombie?"

Josh threw his hands up, walked over to the base of one of the big trees, and sat with his back against its rough bark. Jaden sat down, too, wrapping her arms around her knees and looking at him sideways. Bits of sunlight filtered down through the leaves.

"I wanted to tell you about the Little League World Series," he said. "My dad says I'd be playing against the best of the best in the entire world, but *she* told you before I could."

"I know." Jaden shrugged. "What's up with her? She's your dad's Realtor, or his friend?"

"Supposedly like you and me are friends," Josh said, avoiding Jaden's eyes. "But my mom doesn't think so. They're talking about splitting up."

"Oh," Jaden said, and they sat quietly for a minute. "Is that what she meant about your dad's happiness?"

Josh shrugged. "I guess so."

"Parents can be weird."

"My dad wouldn't even be out looking for a house if it wasn't for me," Josh said.

"That Nike contract is a great thing. Think how bad you wanted it, how hard you worked. Even playing with a cracked bone in your face."

"And this is what I get."

After another pause, Jaden said, "I met a kid named Zamboni Cross once who goes to Grimes. His father was a hockey player or something and named him Zamboni after the ice machine. Maybe this kid is Marcus's brother. He was a little offbeat."

"There could be a whole nest of them for all I care," Josh said. "I didn't even know she had a son, and now I find out that he's playing on the Lyncourt all-star team that my dad thinks I should play on?"

"Wow," Jaden said, "I never even thought about you playing on the all-star team."

"I qualified," Josh said. "All you have to do is play in half the league's regular season games, which I did."

"Can you imagine if you really made it to Williamsport?" Jaden said. "I mean, they'd probably send me to cover it. What a story, a national championship *and* a World Series title?"

"It's a long way from that." Josh scratched his ear. "I don't even know if I want to do this. It takes a whole team to win, and most of these guys haven't even played together before. You see how hard we all work together on the Titans. Who knows if this team could win anything."

"The way you hit the ball? Josh, it's like three automatic runs a game. You're a freak."

"Thanks."

"You know what I mean. Freak in a good way. You know you are. You can see the laces when the ball leaves the pitcher's hand *and* you've got the skill to hit it, wherever it's thrown. Do you know how unusual that is?"

"Lots of baseball players have that," Josh said.

"The great ones," Jaden said. "You're right."

Josh felt his face get hot despite the shade.

"But there's more holding you back than just a raw team," Jaden said, "something you're not telling me."

Josh glanced at her, those big green eyes seeing into him the way they did. He knew the only way to deal with them was to give up something, and something was better than all of it. He was ashamed to even admit it, but Diane's appearance and her message shook him up. If him being away in Albany gave her more opportunities to be around his dad, then Josh didn't want to go, but he was too embarrassed about the whole thing to say that to Jaden.

"I'm not doing this for sure," Josh said. "I told them I wouldn't do it unless Benji can play, too."

"Really?"

"It's a lot of traveling around. My dad will be with the Titans. I just don't feel like doing it by myself."

"I said I might be able to cover it for the paper," Jaden said.

"I know, and that would be great. But, a teammate, you know?"

"Sure."

"Benji's funny," he said.

"No arguments there."

"So, I'm just hoping it works out."

"With your parents, or you mean Benji?" Jaden asked.

"Both," Josh said, rising and dusting off his hands. "Well, I better get it into gear. Batting practice at one. Thanks for swinging by, though."

"I had to get my dad some ink for his printer anyway,"

Jaden said, waving her hand. "Text me when you decide what you're doing. And Josh?"

"Yeah?"

"Congratulations. This could really be great."

Josh got to work but still had to race the mower down the last block, getting home just in time to swap out his green-stained sneakers for his cleats, grab his bat bag, and hop into the front seat of his dad's silver Taurus.

"Set?" Josh's dad asked, starting the engine.

Josh nodded and searched his father's face for signs that he might know Diane had stopped by to see him. His father seemed distracted, though, and Josh tried to figure a way he could bring her up without being obvious. As they drove, Josh's dad switched from station to station on the radio.

Finally Josh said, "You know any of the other kids on this all-star team, Dad?"

"Uh, not really," his dad said without taking his eyes from the road. "Diane's son is on it, I guess."

"Which son?" Josh asked.

"She's only got one," his dad said, shucking a stick of cinnamon gum from its wrapper and stuffing it into his mouth. "Marcus, I think his name is. I haven't met him."

"Not Zamboni?"

His dad chuckled and said, "I think that's the name his father gave him, but Diane calls him Marcus. That's his middle name, but I wouldn't call him Zamboni around her. She's a really nice person, but she's been through a lot."

"Why? You think I'll be around her?" Josh tried to keep the panic out of his voice.

"She's just a friend, Josh," his father said. "But she's been helping me look for a house. We can afford it now, and it's time to get out of the city. The schools are better in the suburbs."

"I like my school," Josh said, not wanting anything to do with moving, especially if it meant his father was going to be with Diane. He remembered Diane saying she and his father had a "real thing" between them, and couldn't help wondering if this was what it all meant. Still, he was unable to bring himself to ask, partly because he felt embarrassed and partly because he was afraid of the answer.

"Yeah, well, you'll like this even better," his dad said. "A man's got to move up in life, Josh. You either go forward or sink backward. You never stay the same. That's life. Your mom, she only wants to stay the same, but it's not possible. And I'm not going backward. I fought for the past twelve years of my life to live a dream I couldn't quite reach. I hope that never happens to you, Josh. I've come to terms with it, and it's time for me to go in a new direction. This time, I'm not going to flounder around."

His father pulled the car into the lot outside the batting cages. Most of Josh's Titans teammates were already there, gathered in a loose cluster around a bench, each with his own bat bag. His father turned off the car and took the keys from the ignition. Josh wondered if, when his dad talked about moving up in life, he had been talking about buying a house or changing his wife. He put a hand on his father's arm and looked up at him.

"Dad," he said, "you can tell me. Are you and Mom getting a divorce?"

CHAPTER SEVEN

HIS FATHER'S LUNGS FILLED and emptied like metal tanks. Finally he jingled the keys and said, "Not now, Josh. The team is waiting. After practice, we'll talk. I promise."

Before Josh could protest, his father pulled his arm free and got out. Josh followed, listening as his dad barked at the team, getting everyone into action at the appropriate stations. Coach Moose did a ball toss drill outside the cages, and that's where Josh began, waiting with Benji while their classmate Kerry Eschelman swung away.

While they stood taking warm-up swings, Josh got to tell Benji all about the all-star team and his plan to get Benji on along with him.

"The best of the best," Benji said, whistling dreamily.

"Man, I can see that happening. It's where we belong, really. Wow. This'll be great, Josh."

"Yeah, I just hope they're okay with you on it."

"Dude, I am so far better than most of the guys in that league," Benji said, tilting his ball cap back on his head. "I'm a Titan, a national champ. Are you kidding? They want to win the World Series, they need a heavy hitter like me. That's a fact. Think about every World Series. You just don't win the big show without a heavy hitter."

"No," Josh said, "I meant because of the eligibility. Remember when you took that trip with your dad? My dad said you have to have played in half the games to qualify. Those are the rules."

Benji's face fell. "I made half, don't you think?"

"I hope so," Josh said. "If it's you and me, this thing could be fun."

Benji was up, then Josh took his turn before continuing on the team's circuit, working down the line of cages on his own, until over an hour later, he finally came to the cage where his dad watched and made adjustments with his players. As he stepped inside the cage, Diane suddenly appeared beside his father. His father grinned from ear to ear. Diane tickled him and his father laughed and gave her a playful shrug. Josh's ears burned. He turned away and stepped into position. He thought he heard his father say the word "sweetie," which made him sick.

When his father told him to get started, Josh didn't

even look back at him. The balls fired at him weren't even close to the ninety-mile-an-hour pitches Josh had hit the night he met Diane, but he could barely see them now. Just the sound of their voices seemed to blur Josh's vision. He swung and missed, over and over, until his father finally noticed.

"Get the weight off that front foot," his father said.

Josh tried to do what he said but missed the next two pitches. In his mind, he could see Diane watching him. He wanted to scream.

"You're not snapping your wrists," his father said. "Focus on your wrists."

Josh nicked one pitch, missed another, and dribbled the rest.

"Let's go, LeBlanc," Josh's dad growled. "Get your head into it. No, don't you go anywhere. You stay here and hit twenty more."

Josh heard a giggle. He glanced over his shoulder and saw Diane walking away. Josh gripped the bat so hard his knuckles turned blue, fighting the urge to hurl it at her.

His father was strict as a dad, but even tougher as a coach. Josh got a full dose of both, partly because it was his dad's nature, and partly, Josh suspected, to show the team that his dad didn't play favorites. But what had just happened had nothing to do with any of that. Josh felt certain that it was about his father acting like a big shot for Diane.

The rest of the team had finished at the other stations, and they clustered outside the cage. Josh tried to focus, but his head was swirling with hatred and rage. After a minute, his father stepped into the cage and tweaked the machine so that the rubber wheels that spit the balls spun faster. The pitches came, red hot, and Josh swung wild, either missing or nicking the ball ineffectively.

"That stinks." His father snapped off the machine. "And don't give me that look. You're distracted? Mind on other things? You want to play in the majors? It's a hundred and sixty-two games a season, and believe me, there'll be distractions all over the board.

"Focus," his father said, pointing at his own eye. "The ones who can't focus, can't play. Go on, get out."

His father raised his voice to the rest of the team. "Okay, you guys. Good work. You've got tomorrow off, but I want everyone ready to go Monday at nine at our field. Full practice, lunch, then another full practice. We need it."

Josh stuffed his bat and gloves into his bag and left the cage while his father picked up the balls himself. Josh's teammates scattered, making their way to their rides in the parking lot. They shied away from Josh, and he knew they felt embarrassed for him. Only Benji remained.

"Dude," Benji said, "that was awful. What happened to you?"

"Thanks," Josh said under his breath. "Some friend."

"What? Friends are honest, right?"

"Sometimes they look at the bright side," Josh said.

"Dude, the only bright spot was you leaving the cage. Come on, don't take it so hard. It's good for everyone else's confidence to see that even the great Josh LeBlanc can have a bad day, too."

"Not according to him," Josh said, angling his head.

"Aw," Benji said, swatting air. "Man's a pussycat."

"What'd you say, Mr. Lido?" Josh's dad squinted at Benji as he left the cage.

"Talking about my cat, Coach," Benji said, beaming at Josh's dad.

"When did you get a cat, Benji?" Josh's dad asked.

"Well, it's really . . . uh . . . the neighbors' cat," Benji said, "but we kind of adopted him. You know my mom, feeding him all the time and letting him in the back. He poops on our bathroom floor, though. My mom says he's trained 'cause he goes in the bathroom, but I say, 'Ma, that is *not* trained.'"

Josh's father nodded silently, slung the bag of balls over his shoulder, and headed for the silver Taurus. Josh and Benji climbed in.

"So, you think they'll let me play, too, Coach?" Benji asked, hanging his hands over the back of the front seat. "I mean, obviously I'm one of the top players, heavy hitter and all that."

Josh's dad glanced in the rearview mirror. "If you

had enough games, they will. I can't keep straight who went to what game. It was baseball every day of the week is all I know, between our practices and tournaments and the Little League games, but didn't you miss an extra game that one time you went with your dad to Niagara Falls? It was Memorial Day, I think."

"Best wax museum on the planet," Benji said. "I showed you guys the picture of me and my dad with Elvis, right?"

"Right," Josh's dad said. "Which is what I'm concerned about. But we'll see."

Coach Q lived in a small red box of a house down a shady side street in Lyncourt. His son, Vito, was on the front lawn playing catch with a kid Josh didn't recognize. It wasn't until they pulled in that Josh saw the white Audi convertible in the driveway tucked up next to the house. Panic boiled up in Josh's stomach, and he looked with wonder at his father.

CHAPTER EIGHT

"IS THAT DIANE'S?" JOSH asked before he could contain the question.

"You mean Ms. Cross?" his dad said.

"Right," Josh said.

"She's the Little League secretary," his dad said. "We need an officer of the league to sign off on the scorebook rosters. That's *if* Benji has played enough games."

Josh nodded and got out. Together they walked to the front step. From the yard, Vito Quatropanni shouted hello. They both knew him from playing on the Delmonico Insurance team together. Vito was short and muscular with olive skin and quick, powerful movements. He could hit and played catcher as well as anyone in the league. Even though his dad was the coach, Vito certainly deserved to be on the all-star team.

The other kid was tall and lanky with sandy blond hair that hung like a mop from beneath his own cap. He turned and, when he saw Josh's dad wasn't looking, stuck a finger in his nose and made a flicking motion toward the driveway. Something flew through the air and landed on the edge of the blacktop. Josh narrowed his eyes at the booger that lay like a jagged meteorite. The kid grinned and went back to his catch.

Benji burst out in a laughing groan. "Dude, that's *Guinness Book of World Records* material."

The kid winked at Benji and gave him a thumbs-up. Benji kept chuckling until Josh nudged him in the ribs.

"Dude? What's that about?" Benji asked.

"What are you laughing at? That was disgusting," Josh said, twisting up his face.

"Take it easy," Benji said. "Gross can be very funny. I still remember when Fletcher Smith puked in Mrs. Malochy's chair in third grade. Remember? She sat down before she smelled it, slipped right off her chair and onto the floor, and then she puked all over Gretchen Carabinno's new red shoes. Stuff like that makes up the bright spots in life."

Josh just shook his head.

Coach Q answered the bell and led them into a small living room, scratching the tufts of hair surrounding his bald head. Beyond the living room, in a tiny kitchen, Diane Cross sat at the square table with her big red purse, a stack of score books, a calculator, and some scraps of paper she had scribbled numbers upon. When she got up, she greeted Josh's dad like a simpering schoolgirl, taking both his hands in her own before kissing him on the cheek. Josh looked away, his face hot with embarrassment. Benji stared with a mouth wide as a largemouth bass's.

"So you're Benji. I'm Diane Cross." She held out her hand. "Josh's father's friend."

"Right," Josh said. "The house saleslady."

"Real estate *agent*," Josh's father said.

Josh's blood went cold. His father gazed at Diane with an expression so silly that it reminded Josh of someone who'd been hit by a pitch.

"Hey, guys." Diane turned her smile from Josh's father to them before her attention shifted back to her calculations. "Your father told me it's important that *both* of you play on the all-stars and I said, 'Of course.' We all know how important team chemistry is, right? Speaking of chemistry, I can't wait until you meet my son. He's an awesome player, and I know you'll all be friends. Everyone loves him."

"I'd say we all got kind of lucky on this," Coach Q said. "The only reason there's room on the roster is because Chris Harrigan and Johnny Sindoni are going on some Rotary exchange. Everyone was supposed to make a commitment for the whole summer. The truth is, I don't think they thought we'd make it to Albany."

"Harrigan and Sindoni?" Benji said. "Imagine how

much better your team's gonna be with us on it instead of them. I can see why they didn't think you'd make it to Albany."

Josh stared at him.

"What?" Benji said. "I'm just saying."

Diane held up a sheet of paper with numbers. "All that doesn't really matter, does it? Like I said, it all comes down to the numbers, and I'm the one who's got them.

"Right here."

CHAPTER NINE

"TWENTY-THREE GAMES IN ALL," Diane said, running her pen down a column of numbers, "including our playoffs. So, you needed twelve. And . . . you've got twelve!"

"Wahoo!" Benji slapped Josh a high five.

"Yes," Josh said, the thrill of having his best friend to travel with overcoming his anxiety for a moment.

"I'll just sign these," Diane said, rifling through the score book and adding her signature to the spots where Benji's name appeared on the roster. Diane slapped the book shut and patted it before rising from the table.

"Okay, Coach," she said. "You got yourself another all-star."

"You got more than an all-star," Benji said, slapping the coach on his back. "Coach, you got yourself a heavy hitter now."

"You don't call Josh a heavy hitter?" Coach Q raised a furry eyebrow.

"Well, he is," Benji said, "but Josh is all about skill, too. When he's not blasting one over the fence, he can put it in the hole or dribble a bunt down the third-base line. With me, it's all or nothing, Coach. I'm as heavy as they come."

Coach Q chuckled and informed them that they'd be hitting the road first thing Monday morning.

"We'll meet at Grant Middle at seven-thirty," Coach Q said. "As long as we keep winning, we'll be in Albany for the sectional finals all week, so pack for five days. After Albany—presuming we can beat everybody there—we'll go to New Jersey for the regional finals. If we win in the regionals, it's hello, Williamsport, and the World Series."

"Who else is in this show?" Benji asked. "We got some pitchers, right?"

"You got Niko Fedchenko," Coach Q said, "and the Fries brothers, Callan and Camren."

Benji whistled. "Not bad, Coach. You done good."

"And Marcus! Marcus in left field," Diane said, looking eagerly at Josh's dad. "He really came into his own this season. It's really amazing."

"Marcus is a fine player," Josh's dad said, nodding and grinning at Diane, who just about melted at his words.

Josh nudged Benji and said, "Let's get out of here."

He and Benji left the adults to talk. Outside, Vito and his buddy were nowhere to be seen.

"Hopefully that kid with the booger was just from the neighborhood," Benji said, looking around, "and not on our all-star team."

"Yeah, but you know what my dad says," Josh said. "A team isn't a social club, Benji. Sometimes you have to come together as a team with people you wouldn't normally be friends with. That's how you win. That's baseball."

"Team, shmeam. You and me are the franchise. How many other teams in this shindig you think will have two national champs on their roster? About zilch."

"Benji," Josh said. "I know you like to kid around, but seriously, you know as well as me that you gotta have a complete team to get to the World Series."

"Good thing I had enough games," Benji said. "How about that? We were all worried for nothing."

"It wasn't nothing," Josh said. "I only made it by one game, and you missed that Memorial Day weekend game. You didn't tell me you played a game that I wasn't at."

"Dude," Benji said. "I never played when you weren't there."

"But she said you had twelve." Josh's words trailed off. "She must have made a mistake."

He reached for the doorknob.

"Dude," Benji said, grabbing Josh's wrist, "are you

nuts? Leave it alone. I'm on the team, right? Her mistake is our chance to play in the World Series."

"I know, but—"

"Dude, the only butt is your face," Benji said. "Cut it out. She said I've got enough to play, just leave it alone. If it's an honest mistake, who cares? That's life. Look at Cinderella."

"Cinderella?"

"Yeah, she drops the glass slipper, right? Big mistake. But if she doesn't drop that sucker, she's sweepin' ashes for the rest of her life. Get it?"

"But I think Diane did it on purpose, Benji," Josh said. "I mean, of course I want you to play. I told my dad I wasn't doing it without you."

"Which is probably why she did it," Benji said. "She wants the heavy hitters on the team so her ice-machine son can win a trophy. I can't blame her."

The door opened and Josh's dad almost knocked them over.

"You guys ready?" he asked. "Let's go."

Josh said nothing more about it. They dropped Benji off at his mom's and went home. Josh couldn't remember a more bizarre day in his life. He had so many questions, so many concerns, but one overpowered them all. Josh's dad pulled into the garage and cut the motor.

"Dad," Josh said, part of him not wanting to talk, but the other part knowing that he wouldn't be able to think about anything else unless he knew. "You said we could talk after practice."

"You call that practice?" His dad glared at him.

"I know you're not that mad at my batting," Josh said quietly.

His father's face softened, and his shoulders sagged a bit.

"No," he said, speaking slow and deliberate. "You're right. I'm not. I mean, I was mad at your batting. I meant what I said about having to be able to put your mind above the distractions. I'm serious, Josh. That's critical. But I'm more mad about my life. Where I've been. Where I *haven't* been.

"Josh, I'm getting my own apartment. I'm moving out."

"Oh, Dad," Josh said, tears spilling instantly down his cheeks. His father's face blurred beyond recognition.

When his father's enormous hand clamped down on his shoulder and squeezed, Josh buried his face in his arm to stifle the sobs.

CHAPTER TEN

JOSH'S DAD DIDN'T STAY. He went upstairs and came down dressed in slacks and a button-down shirt. Under his arm was the briefcase he'd begun to carry around, stuffed with materials on home listings, tax maps, and builders' marketing information. When Josh's mom saw him, the spoon she'd been mixing with clattered into the sink. She hurried out the door, wiping her hands on her apron without looking back. Josh's dad stared after her a second. He kissed Laurel—who was busy with a stack of blocks on the kitchen floor—then the top of Josh's head.

His dad wouldn't meet Josh's eyes. "I'll be back later to pick up some things."

Josh watched him go without a word. The door shut and Laurel began to cry.

"Don't worry," Josh said, scooping her up off the kitchen floor. "He'll come back. You want to play cats and dogs?"

Laurel bobbed her head vigorously and almost immediately stopped crying, trading her sobs for barking noises. Josh put her down, got on all fours, and began to meow. Then he let her chase him all around the house, nipping at his heels until she had him cornered and he turned on her, spitting and hissing, and used his cat's claws to tickle her until she cried a different kind of tear. Josh laughed, too, infected by her silly glee.

When he heard the back door open, Josh looked up from the living room floor and watched his mom come back in. Her red and swollen eyes stared dully at Josh. She crooked her finger at him, telling him to come to the kitchen. When he got there, his mom offered Laurel a Barney DVD along with her binkie, a pink silky blanket worn thin from love.

After his mom set Laurel up in the TV room, she returned to the kitchen.

"Sit down, honey," she said.

She slipped on a baking mitt and removed a warm-smelling tray of sugar cookies from the oven and laid it on the table. Each of the cookies stared up at him with a Cyclops raisin eye. His mom poured a tall, cold glass of milk and put it in front of him.

"I'm not hungry, Mom," Josh said.

"Cookies make you feel better whether you're hungry

or not." She sat down beside him. "Go ahead."

Josh picked one up, blew on it a bit, then ate out its eye.

"These things happen," his mom began. "People fight."

Josh hung his head.

"You're growing up," she said. "You're almost a man, Josh. Look at you. I don't want this to spoil things for you. You have so much waiting, things your father and I never got to do."

Josh thought his tears had been spent, but he broke a new bank and they coursed down his cheeks as he looked up at her.

"I'm going to win everything and give it all to you," he said. "I'm going to buy you the biggest house on the planet and a Bentley. I'm going to buy you a three-hundred-foot yacht."

His mom tilted her head, looking even sadder. She reached over to take his hand and spoke softly to him.

"I taught you better than that," she said, "didn't I? You know all those things aren't what matters. No, don't be ashamed. You're young and your father, well, those things mean something to him, and you can't help feeling that way. You've got a lot of your father in you, Josh, that hunger to be the best, and the baseball part, the arm and the eye and that awesome swing. But you've got me in you, too. The part that knows you don't have to have money to watch the sunset drop like a cherry fireball, or to laugh like you just did with your little sister. Those things don't cost money; you just have to be smart enough to know they're there for you, and to enjoy them. Don't be fooled because your father is running around talking about new homes and cars and clothes. I don't need *things*. I just need you and Laurel."

"What about Dad?" Josh was still crying quietly. "Don't you need him, too?"

His mom covered her mouth and nodded sharply.

"I do," she said, nearly choking on her words. "But two out of three is better than a lot of people get, and you have to look at what you have, not what you've lost. Besides, you never know what's going to happen.

"Listen, enough about me. I want to talk about you. Now, with everything going on, I need to stay here and look for a job, but I want you to go to this tournament in Albany and have *fun*. I mean it. Play baseball. Forget about all this and enjoy being twelve and an all-star. Believe me, it's the best thing you can do for me."

Josh looked at her and said, "I'll try, Mom. I don't know if I can, but I'll try."

CHAPTER ELEVEN

JOSH WAS RELIEVED WHEN Jaden and her dad invited him and Benji to spend Sunday with them out on Skaneateles Lake. Jaden's dad—a doctor in residence at St. Joseph's Hospital—had rented a party boat at the Skaneateles Marina for the day. The summer sun baked the earth, water, and sky, but out on the boat with a gentle breeze and a cooler full of sodas and iced teas and the water just a leap away, the day was like heaven. Jaden's dad took them into the town for lunch, mooring the boat at the public docks. They walked around, looking into the shops before eating thick, juicy hamburgers at Johnny Angel's Heavenly Hamburgers, then polishing off their meals with triple ice-cream cones from the Blue Water Chill.

Jaden's dad told them he'd meet them at the boat,

and the three of them watched a colony of martins swooping and shrieking, picking bugs out of the air before landing on an ancient white birdhouse to feed their young. When Jaden's father returned, he had two boxes of donuts from the Skaneateles Bakery under his arm and a cappuccino in his hand.

"You'll thank me later," he said, setting the boxes down on the seat before unmooring the boat.

They stayed until the sun winked away over the rolling hills of farmland, thankful for the donuts that kept Benji breathing until they could stop for fish sandwiches at Doug's Fish Fry on their way back through town. By the time he got back, Josh was too exhausted to fret over his parents, and the sight of his mom sitting alone reading a book in her chair left only a dull ache in his chest. He kissed her and hugged her tight without a word, then climbed into bed, falling asleep instantly.

Monday morning Josh's alarm didn't go off, and he had to scramble to get ready. His father pulled into the driveway, picked Josh up, and dropped him off at the middle school with nothing more than a gruff "Good luck." Josh stepped up into the bus, taking the seat just behind Coach Q, where Benji waited. Benji asked him what was wrong, but Josh waved him off, said he had a stomachache, and shut his eyes tight, pretending to sleep. The bus geared up and headed east on the thruway.

Ten miles before Albany, Coach Q announced that when they got to the hotel, their keys would be waiting for them in envelopes with their names on them on a table inside the door. They should each get unpacked and meet, ready to go get warmed up for their first game, a half hour after they arrived. Josh's being out of sorts hadn't dampened Benji's spirits at all. When they pulled up in front of the Holiday Inn Express, Benji called dibs on using the bathroom first and bolted off the bus, telling Josh he'd see him in the room.

Josh grabbed his bags from the underbelly of the bus, found the envelope with his key, and went to the room. He didn't bother unpacking but simply tossed the big duffel bag on top of the dresser and flopped down on the bed by the window, covering his eyes with his arm and trying not to think about the mess he'd left behind him. More than anything, he wanted to get out onto the field and play. Just play, and forget about it all.

The doorknob rattled.

"Couldn't make it to the bathroom in the room, huh?" Josh said from beneath the crook in his arm as the door burst open and crashed into the wall. "Take it easy, Lido, we're here all week."

"Whatever you say, chicken livers. But this is my crib, too, and you ain't my momma. Let's get that straight right off."

"Chicken what?" Josh said, sitting up.

The face that grinned back at him wasn't Benji's.

CHAPTER TWELVE

"**WHAT ARE *YOU* DOING** here? Who are you?" Josh asked.

The kid from outside of Vito Quatropanni's house grinned. "I'm your new roomie, Roomie."

"Yeah, I doubt that," Josh said. "Lido's my roomie. It's in my contract, slob."

"Well, my mom does all the contracts for this circus and she's the one who put me with you, so your credibility with me is already in the crapper. You'll have to earn my trust back, that's all."

"Dude." Josh stood up. "I'm so serious. Who the heck *are* you?"

The kid bowed dramatically. "I am the Great Zamboni. Feel the power."

Josh's mouth fell open. "The Great . . . Zamboni? Your mom's the real estate lady?"

Zamboni shoved Josh's duffel bag off the edge of the dresser top to make room for his own.

"That's my stuff," Josh said.

"Yeah," Zamboni said, "on my dresser. You can use the one over there by the window."

"Okay." Josh bit the inside of his mouth and clenched his fists. "We're not going to have to worry about this because there is no way this is happening."

He stormed out of the room and took the stairs down to the lobby, where he found Coach Q.

"Coach," he said, trying to stay calm, "there's a mistake with my room. I'm supposed to be with Lido, Benji, my friend."

Coach Q wore his purple Lyncourt cap and a gray uniform with matching purple trim that stretched over his big gut. He looked up from his clipboard, removed his aviator sunglasses, and squinted at Josh.

"Look, Josh," he said. "I know we all scrambled to get you here, and we're pumped up to have you. We can win this thing with you on the roster. But do you really want to act like this? I mean, your friend had to be on the team, fine. He's not terrible. But now you want to start rearranging the rooming list half an hour before we leave for our first game? Like you're king of the castle here? Really? What do you think your dad would say?"

Coach Q stared at Josh. Josh felt his insides melt into a puddle of shame. He hung his head.

"No, Coach," he said. "I'm sorry. You're right. I didn't mean it like that."

"If you didn't mean it like that, then I guess you'll figure a way to just get along with Marcus, right?"

"Marcus?"

"Cross."

"He calls himself Zamboni," Josh said.

Coach Q winced and looked around. "You don't want to call him that around the mom. He's Marcus to me and the coaches. That's it, and you'll save everybody a lot of headache if you remember."

"But he calls himself that," Josh said.

Coach Q raised his hands in surrender and shook his head. "Please."

"Fine," Josh said.

"Thanks, Josh. Go get changed."

Josh didn't feel like taking the stairs, so he pushed the button and waited for the elevator. When it slid open, Benji stood there with Vito Quatropanni, sharing a bag of Nacho Cheese Doritos.

"Hey, Josh," Benji said, "what's up?"

"You two are rooming together?" Josh asked.

"Yeah," Benji said, grinning and raising the bag of chips. "Vito's loaded up with junk. I guess I'm the perfect guy to help him out, you know?"

Josh pushed past them on his way into the elevator. Benji turned as he got off.

"Hey," Benji said cheerfully, "what's wrong?"

"Nothing," Josh said as the doors began to close. "Don't choke on your chips. I'll see you on the bus."

As the doors waggled closed, Benji told Vito, "He gets moody sometimes, but it's a good thing. That's how he was when we took the national title."

Back in the room, Zamboni lay on the bed fully dressed for the game, his cleats hanging off the edge of the covers, hat on his head.

"Back, huh?" Zamboni said, smacking a mouthful of gum.

"Guess so," Josh said, hauling his bag up from the floor and resting it atop the dresser by the window before changing into his uniform.

The window was open, and a breeze wafted the curtains. As he changed, Josh sniffed the air.

"Did you smoke a cigarette or something?" Josh asked.

"Can it, Scarface," Zamboni said.

Josh touched the scar on his face from a surgery he'd had to repair a broken eye socket so he could play in the Hall of Fame National Championship. It was still a raised, angry red line beneath his eye, but most people didn't mention it. Josh glared for a moment at Zamboni, then shook his head. As he pulled off his T-shirt, Josh heard a soft thwack against the mirror. When his head popped out through the collar, the sight of a thick and blood-streaked booger on the glass made his stomach heave. Retching, Josh dashed for the bathroom, aware of Zamboni's explosion of laughter from the bed.

Josh splashed cold water on his face and let his stomach settle. As he stood leaning over the sink, he heard the sound of Zamboni laughing as he left the room, leaving the door wide-open. Benji, who was passing by with Vito, popped into the room to see what was so funny.

"It's one of the sickest things I've ever seen," Josh said from the bathroom. "Right on the mirror in there."

Josh heard Benji come in, then hoot with laughter before he said, "Vito, come check this out. Man, this thing is, like, out of a horror movie. It's like an alien or something. I think it's got a pulse. How awesome is that?"

"Man," Vito said, "don't touch it, Benji."

"He touched it?" Josh said half to himself as he peered around the corner to see Benji poking the specimen stuck to the mirror.

Josh bolted back to the sink and dry heaved. Benji howled even harder and patted Josh on the back before he headed out with Vito. Josh heard their chatter fade as they made their way down the hall, Benji obviously unaware that Josh was mad at him.

Josh spit in the sink and looked at himself in the bathroom mirror, wondering what he was doing there, and, even if they could make it all the way to the World Series, if it could possibly be worth it.

CHAPTER THIRTEEN

JOSH GOT OFF THE bus without waiting for Benji. He carried his bat bag into the dugout. He leaned his bat against the wall and pulled the mitt onto his hand. The feel and smell of the leather comforted him and put a lift in his step as he hopped out onto the field.

He breathed in the smell of grass and dirt and pressed his glove against his nose, inhaling deeply. On the adjacent field, the sounds of another game already in progress floated his way: the crack of a bat, the smack of a ball thrown from third to first, the bellow of a coach, and cheers from the crowd.

Josh watched his teammates during warm-ups, making mental notes on small things his father would point out if he was the coach. In the bright sunshine, he began to feel better. Coach Q peppered the ball around the infield, calling out situations and looking for the correct reactions as he prepped his team.

"Man on second," Coach Q shouted, smashing a grounder between Josh and third.

Josh scrambled and snatched up the ball, pausing for a moment and looking pointedly at second before firing the ball to first.

"You gotta get it there, LeBlanc," Coach Q hollered. "Come on, you're supposed to be our superstar."

Josh opened his mouth to remind the coach that he'd said a runner was on second and that Josh needed to check that runner to keep him from advancing before he made the throw to first. But he remembered the coach's words at the hotel about reporting Josh to his dad, so he kept quiet. It made him feel like more bad things were yet to come.

"Hey," Benji said, sliding in behind him in line to run bases. "I'm sorry about the Doritos. I should have offered you some."

"You think I'm mad about the Doritos?" Josh asked.

"You aren't?"

"I thought we'd be rooming together. Doesn't it bother you?"

"Well," Benji said, "sure, but I didn't want to make Vito feel bad. He's okay."

"If he's okay, he wouldn't be hanging around with that Zamboni."

"Marcus?"

"Whatever you want to call him. He's no one I want to room with. Did you know he smokes?"

"I asked Vito about him," Benji said. "He said Marcus is a little wacko. They're not really friends. His mom just dumps him off sometimes. She wants him to have friends. That's what Vito told me. Vito's okay."

"You already told me what a swell guy Vito is," Josh said, annoyed.

"Oh. Right. Well," Benji said, quickly stringing his words together. "Hey, we can still hang together, right? I mean, it's you and me. Franchise material. Champs. Pride of Syracuse. All that. Hey, it's game time, brother."

Josh couldn't help but smile. "Yeah," he said. "Me and you. Let's do this thing. I'm tired of all the drama. I want to play some doggone baseball. You know what I mean, Benji?"

Benji put a hand on Josh's shoulder. "Exactly."

After the Lyncourt team cleared the field, they had the chance to watch their opponents warm up. Josh sat on the end of the bench, as far from Zamboni as he could get. Benji sat next to him, and Vito next to Benji.

"Where are these guys from?" Benji asked Vito.

Vito cleared his throat and spit into the dirt. "I think Gloversville."

"They look like glovers," Benji said. "Little guys. Little glovers."

"Don't get too cute," Josh said, narrowing his eyes at the pitcher. "That kid on the mound is throwing the cover off the ball."

"They come in fast, I send 'em out far," Benji said.

Vito nodded.

"And he's got a changeup, too," Josh said. "You better pay attention. He gives it away, watch."

"Watch what?" Benji said.

"That was a fastball," Josh said. "Watch to see if he throws another changeup. Watch his head. See that?"

The pitcher threw a changeup, the same windup to deliver a lob ball with no heat.

"See what?" Benji said, kicking the dirt.

"That little twitch," Josh said. "He does it at the back of his windup. You see it, Vito?"

"I don't see nothing," Vito said.

"My man has eagle eyes," Benji said, patting Josh on the back. "Part of his skill set."

"You better watch," Josh said.

"I got this guy in my sights." Benji aimed his finger like a pistol. "These guys are just a warm-up, a snack."

Coach Q called out to stand for the National Anthem.

"Okay," Josh said, leaving the dugout. "Don't say I didn't warn you."

The first three Lyncourt batters went up and down. The undersized Gloversville pitcher only had to throw thirteen pitches to do it. Josh watched the last guy go down from the on-deck circle, then swapped his batting glove and helmet for his mitt before finding his spot at shortstop.

Josh's team had a good pitcher, too. Niko Fedchenko was a lefty with a wicked curveball as well as a knuckleball that gave Gloversville fits. He walked one batter and the infield gave up another runner when the third baseman committed an error, but two batters popped out and Fedchenko sent a third down swinging. Josh clapped his hands as he headed for the dugout, getting geared up to hit. His head felt light and his heart thumped against the inside of his chest like a marching band's bass drum. This was what he loved. Baseball. Sunshine. The mild sour stench of his sweat-stained batting glove. Matching his eye and bat against a good pitcher.

Josh stepped up to the plate.

The pitcher went into his windup.

Josh narrowed his eyes and reared back, ready.

He couldn't believe what he saw.

CHAPTER FOURTEEN

JOSH KNEW EVEN BEFORE the ball left the pitcher's hand that it would be impossible to hit. He knew it just by the angle of the pitcher's arm as it whiplashed forward from behind his right ear. The catcher jumped away from the plate and the ball hit his glove with a smack. Josh couldn't help stepping out of the box to take a curious glance at the Gloversville coach in his dugout.

The coach clapped his hands and nodded his head at the pitcher.

"That's it," the coach said.

"That's it?" Josh said under his breath. Stepping into the box, he studied the pitcher, who offered up an awkward smile.

The next pitch came the same way, so far outside the plate that the catcher could barely get it. Josh grit his

teeth and shook his head, offering a look of frustration to Coach Q. The coach nodded, like having Josh intentionally walked was all okay. Well, it wasn't okay with Josh.

He staggered his stance and crouched just a bit lower. When the pitch came, Josh sprang across the plate and swung, clipping the ball and sending it screaming off his bat, a foul line drive that nearly mashed Coach Q's front teeth.

"Josh!" the coach cried when he had recovered himself and straightened his cap. "If he's going to give you the base, take it!"

Josh opened his mouth to shout right back. Everyone stared. Coach Q obviously didn't know the game like Josh's father, but thinking of his own father also reminded Josh of the discipline he had learned. He knew better than to back talk a coach, even an inadequate one. Josh stepped up to the plate. The catcher went even wider from the plate, and the pitcher threw the next two well out of Josh's reach. Josh jogged down the baseline to first with the inside of his lip firmly clenched between his teeth to keep from saying something he'd regret.

This wasn't baseball. This was a joke.

Josh then begged the first-base coach to let him steal.

"Coach," he said, "I can make it to third in two pitches, and then, just one bad pitch and I'll get us a run."

But when the coach signaled the dugout, asking for

the go-ahead to send Josh, Coach Q called him off.

The next three batters went down swinging, including Benji. Josh returned to the dugout and had to do everything he could not to throw his helmet and yell at Coach Q, who stood checking his BlackBerry while he chewed on a wad of gum.

Josh sidled up to Benji and said into his ear, "Does this guy want to win or what?"

Benji shrugged.

"I mean, he wouldn't let me hunt those pitches. I was begging to steal, and they wouldn't let me do that either."

"Maybe they just don't know what you can do," Benji said. "That first foul almost killed the guy."

"Well, you gotta swing to hit it, right?" Josh said.

"That's what I was doing," Benji said, thumbing his own chest. "But dude, you were right, he's slick as a watermelon seed."

"Just watch his eyes in the middle of his windup. If he twitches, it's that changeup. If he doesn't do it, it's all heat. That's your pitch, right?"

"Oh yeah," Benji said. "I just gotta see that twitch. I will."

"Good," Josh said, "because if they keep intentionally walking me, someone has to get something or we're done."

"Well." Benji shrugged. "We'll just go back to the Titans, right?"

"Benji," Josh said, "we didn't do this for a free bus ride to Albany. We want to make it to Williamsport. Can you imagine? Players from all over the world. The best of the best. They won't be intentionally walking me there."

"So, what do we do?" Benji asked.

Josh punched his glove. "First thing we do is play defense. If they can't score, they can't win. Come on."

Defense they played.

Josh dove and hustled and threw, accounting for at least one out in every inning. Gloversville didn't have any great bats, but as Fedchenko wore down, they began to knick away at Lyncourt with a single here, a double there, and a handful of walks. When Coach Q pulled Fedchenko, Josh knew they had to score and score fast. The relief pitcher Coach Q put in was Callan Fries. Josh remembered Callan and his brother Camren from some of the Little League games. Josh recalled how Callan killed them for an inning and a half but then faded fast. He was a classic relief pitcher who wouldn't do them any good if he had to throw extra innings. And, Josh knew, if they won, they'd need Camren fresh for tomorrow. Even though they had six players who could pitch, after Fedchenko and the Fries brothers the rest of the pitching wasn't as strong.

As his team approached the dugout in the top of the sixth, Josh shook his head.

"I don't know," he said to Benji, "we don't score now, I

don't think we win. I wish that guy would go at me, just once. Man, would I smack that thing out of this park."

"Hey." Benji snapped his fingers. "I got an idea."

"Nothing crazy, right?"

"No, not crazy for you," Benji said. "Me, on the other hand? Well, I'm glad my mom's not here, that's all I can say. What I'm about to do could get ugly."

CHAPTER FIFTEEN

JOSH PULLED ON HIS batting glove and helmet. He warmed up his shoulders and arms in the batting circle, preparing himself even though he doubted a single pitch would come his way that he could swing at. Benji turned his cap backward and sauntered out to the first-base line.

"Hey!" Benji shouted at the pitcher, who pretended not to notice Benji as he warmed up. "Yeah, you. Half-pint."

The pitcher's head snapped around and he glared.

"Oh, you don't like being a little man?" Benji said, tilting his head in a clownish manner. "It's okay, little fella, that's our *short*stop. It's sad, dude. You're actually a pretty decent pitcher. But I guess a tiny tot like you just has to be afraid of someone as tall as my man."

Benji jerked his thumb toward Josh.

Josh's stomach twisted.

"Benji," Josh said under his breath. "Cut that out."

"What?" Benji called out, raising his eyebrows and spreading his fingers across his chest. "Oh, I get it, Josh. You don't want to scare the little fella any more than he already is. I know. We don't want to see a big yellow pee stain on those white pants he's wearing. It's okay, little guy, you don't have to pitch to the big boys. We understand. Don't cry."

"Benji!" Coach Q shouted from the dugout. "Stop jabbering to the other team and sit down."

Benji turned toward the dugout.

"Don't be afraid to lay it on a little yourself," Benji said, winking at Josh as he went past.

Josh stepped into the batter's box, wiggled his feet into the dirt, took a couple swings, and reared back, ready in case. The pitcher went into his windup and threw a ball six feet outside the plate. The Gloversville coach clapped his hands.

Benji hooted and hollered from the dugout like a mad clown. "Ha ha ha! Look how scared he is! Watch his pants! Yellow stain! Yellow stain!"

Josh felt his own face blush, and he was relieved to hear Coach Q bark at Benji to be quiet or he'd toss him out of the park.

"Okay, Coach," Benji said, as cheerful as if the coach had asked him if he'd like a stick of gum.

The next pitch came, this time not so far outside.

Benji howled with laughter.

"Benji!" Coach Q shouted.

"I didn't say anything," Benji said, "but I can't help laughing, Coach. It's too funny."

The pitcher now gritted his teeth so tight that the cords stood out in his neck. He shook his head at the catcher and gave a silent signal.

"Uh-uh," the catcher said.

"Yes," the pitcher said through his teeth.

Without any more debate, the pitcher wound up and threw one right down the pipe, all heat.

Josh was caught off guard, and in the instant it took the ball to reach the plate, Saturday's scene in the batting cage with his father replayed itself in his head, filling him with doubt.

Uncertain and unprepared—but knowing it might be the only pitch he got—Josh swung with everything he had.

CHAPTER SIXTEEN

THE CRACK OF THE bat was like the split of a campfire stone.

Even Josh gasped.

The ball took off, flying so far beyond the fence that the center fielder moved nothing but his head as he watched it go.

The Lyncourt dugout burst into cheers. As Josh rounded the bases with a silly grin on his face, Gloversville's red-faced coach blasted his pitcher for throwing to Josh. After being mobbed by his teammates, Josh plunked himself down next to Benji, thrilled with the run but not completely comfortable with what they had to do to get it.

Benji held a hand out for Josh to slap him five. Josh just looked at it.

"Come on, you Boy Scout. We each have our own special talents," Benji said. "I did my part, and you did yours."

"I like scoring, but jawing at the guy like that? I don't know."

"Jawing is part of the game," Benji said, "and you'll like it if we win this thing, won't you? Coming all this way to watch some chump intentionally walk you? Come on. That kid deserves it for being a sissy."

"You're right," Josh said. "That's garbage. Play the game, right? Although I guess he was doing what his coach told him to do."

Benji swatted at the air dismissively. "Maybe it'll teach him that you can't always listen to your coach."

"Just don't say that around my dad," Josh said.

"Hey, if you'd listened to that Coach Valentine? You would have been taking steroids."

Josh sighed and said, "When you're right, you're right."

"It's not easy being right all the time," Benji said, punching Josh's shoulder. "But I'm used to it."

The Gloversville pitcher put the next three Lyncourt batters down with nine straight, burning strikes. With each out, he glared over at Josh and Benji.

"Hey!" Benji shouted to his teammates as they took the field. "Don't get distracted, boys. Josh got us our run, but we gotta close these guys out. Defense. Defense. Defense!"

Josh bumped fists with his friend and took up his spot at shortstop. Callan started out the inning hot. He threw a curve that the first batter swung at and missed. The Lyncourt chatter—led by Benji out in right field—began to grow stronger. Callan threw a fastball that the batter sent foul outside the first-base line. The next pitch went wild, but the fourth—another fastball—left the first batter kicking the dirt. The chatter picked up even more.

Callan put the next batter down and Benji went wild, hooting and shrieking praises from right field like a madman. The third batter got up and swung at a curveball, missing.

"World Series. World Series. World Series," Benji began to chant.

Benji was on a roll.

Callan seemed nervous, and he threw three balls to prove it—wild pitches all over the map. The chatter faded. Callan looked over at Josh, who offered a thumbs-up and a nod of encouragement.

"You can do this, Cal!" Josh shouted.

Callan nodded and let a fastball fly. The batter swung and missed, making it a 3–2 count.

"You got it now, Callan!" Benji screamed from right field. "This one is in the bag. He can't hit it! He can't hit it! This thing is over! This thing is ours!"

That's when things fell apart.

CHAPTER SEVENTEEN

JOSH GLANCED BACK AT Benji—wanting to signal to his friend not to jinx them by saying this thing was over—when he heard the crack of the bat. He hadn't even seen Callan throw the pitch. By the time Josh swung his head around, a worm-burner had already ripped through the infield between him and the third baseman. Josh scrambled for it but wasn't even close. He chased the ball into left field, veering out of the way as Zamboni scooped it up and made a wild throw to second, where the batter was already headed. The throw sailed over the second baseman. Benji lurched toward the overthrow, late to the backup.

Josh saw what was happening. He knew the limits of Benji's arm and that the pitcher wasn't moving into position for the cutoff to home plate. Josh took off. Benji heaved the ball toward home plate and it sailed like a lame duck. Josh ran under it, though, snatching it from the air, even as he realized the runner had rounded third and was on his way home.

Josh rotated his hips and fired for home plate. The ball snapped into Vito's mitt at the plate, but he dropped it. The runner reversed his direction anyway. Vito recovered as Josh sprinted toward him, holding up both hands and shouting at him to hold the ball.

"Just hold it!" Josh said, afraid of another overthrow and knowing the chances of getting the runner out were slim to none.

Flustered, Vito handed the ball to Josh, nodding his head. Josh checked the runner, who huffed and puffed atop third. Josh then tossed it underhand to Callan Fries.

"It's okay," Josh said, speaking in a low, confident tone to the pitcher as he returned to his spot at short-stop. "You can do this, Callan. One more out."

Callan Fries nodded, but Josh could see the tremble in his hand. He was shaken, and proved it by walking the next batter, throwing only a single strike when the batter took a swing at a mile-high pitch. It had happened. The relief pitcher had spent everything he had.

Josh looked at Coach Q, waiting for him to come to the mound and make a switch. Callan had done his part; now they might as well use up Camren. What sense was there saving one of his top pitchers? If they lost, there'd be no other game. Coach Q looked out over the field, chomping on his gum, his eyes hidden behind dark sunglasses as he cheered Callan on. Josh opened his mouth but realized there was nothing he could do.

Callan nodded at Vito, the catcher, wound up, and threw a pitch that Vito had to dive for. Josh grit his teeth and clenched his hands, willing Coach Q to see what he saw. Callan walked the batter, loading up the bases.

"You can do it," Coach Q shouted.

Josh moved toward the mound.

"Cal," Josh said. "Callan! Listen to me. Don't worry about striking him out. Just lob it in, buddy. Let us do the rest. Let him hit it. We got a good D. We can get him. Just relax and throw it in nice and easy."

Callan looked doubtfully over at Josh.

"You got it?" Josh asked.

Callan nodded.

"Okay." Josh moved back into his position.

Callan wound up and lobbed one in, nice and easy, but a strike. The batter reared back and swung for the fence. The bat cracked, and Josh winced as the ball took off. There was nothing he could do but watch it sail for the right field fence. Part of him felt relief that the whole thing would be over and he'd be back home where he just might somehow help his parents stay together. The other part of him knew that the rift between his parents had grown too wide for him to fix, and he felt bitter disappointment that he'd never get to Williamsport and play against the best of the best.

Either way, it was out of Josh's hands. Benji backpedaled like his life was on the line.

The ball floated high, then began to drop.

Benji stumbled.

One arm spun like a pinwheel as Benji crashed to the ground with an outstretched glove.

CHAPTER EIGHTEEN

"HOOT, HOOT, HOOTENANNY!" BENJI cried as he slowly rose from the grass, lifting the ball from his glove for the world to see. "Wahoooooo!"

Benji did a little leap, then sprinted toward the infield—the ball still held high—to meet the rush of cheering teammates as they swarmed him for the game-saving catch. In the carnival of admiration, Josh found his friend. He held the back of Benji's head and mashed their foreheads together, noses nearly touching and screaming their lungs out as they hopped about in the eye of the victory storm.

On the bus ride back to the hotel, Callan let the other players know about Josh's coaching him on the mound.

"I'm telling you," Callan told a bunch of eager faces around him, "it went down exactly like Josh said. He told me to just let the guy hit it, that our defense would make a play. We were toast if it wasn't for Josh."

Josh felt his face heat up, but he enjoyed the praise, and when Camren asked if Josh could watch him pitch the next day and give him any pointers he thought of, Josh felt like maybe the whole all-star thing might work out fine after all. He joined in with the others, teasing Benji about falling to the ground when he made the big catch. Benji played right along with it, and in the laughter Josh didn't even think about how disappointed he was to be rooming with Zamboni.

The break in his discomfort didn't last long. Josh hadn't been back in his hotel room for ten minutes before Zamboni came in smelling like cigarette smoke.

"How do you do that to yourself?" Josh asked.

"What?"

"Smoke."

"I don't smoke," Zamboni said. "Mind your own business."

"I can smell it on you," Josh said. "And I know you smoked in the room when I wasn't here."

"Smell this," Zamboni said, lifting his leg with a wet, ripping sound.

So loud and fantastic was the sound that Josh couldn't help from bursting out laughing, even as he covered his nose with one arm. Zamboni looked suspiciously at him for a minute, then smiled crookedly and said, "Smells like bologna."

"Aw, gross," Josh said. "I thought I got away from that stuff without Benji."

"If you were in a tight place, you'd want to come out, too," Zamboni said. "Sounds like Benji is a man after my own heart."

"You both have special skills, I'll say that," Josh said.

"That Benji's okay," Zamboni said. "I'm glad my mom got him on the team."

"What do you mean?" Josh asked, remembering how the number of games shouldn't have added up for Benji to qualify.

"Yeah," Zamboni said. "Who do you think fudged the score books? He didn't have enough games to be on the all-star team."

"Why did she do that? I mean, I'm glad she did and all, but . . ."

Zamboni shrugged. "You were the one who said you wouldn't play without Benji. She just made it happen. I know we don't like each other, but even I gotta admit it, without you, we wouldn't have won today. I'm glad she did it, from a baseball perspective."

Josh looked at Zamboni, unsure exactly how he felt, and said, "But not like a friend thing, right?"

CHAPTER NINETEEN

ZAMBONI STUDIED HIM FOR a moment before he said, "I think my mom put us together because she has some stupid idea about us all being one big happy family. That's a joke. We're not family; we're not even friends."

"I'm hearing that," Josh said.

"But the baseball part of it," Zamboni said, "that might be okay."

"What do you mean?" Josh asked.

"I mean that if you see something that can help me the way you helped Callan? Just tell me."

"Like, coach you?" Josh asked.

"I don't need you *coaching* me," Zamboni said. "You're a kid, like me. Just a tip. If you see one. That's all."

Josh nodded, and the next day, as they warmed up

for their game against a team from Lowville, he did see something. It was early morning. Dew from a cool night still clung to the grass, and a chill squeezed goose bumps to the surface of Josh's bare arms. Coach Q began peppering them with grounders.

After a few, Coach Q said, "Men on first and second."

He then sent a high-bouncing grounder just past the third baseman, who quickly recovered and got to his bag. Zamboni was in left field and he attacked the ball, stopping it with his glove, but not cleanly. Zamboni reared back and zipped the ball high to third base. The third baseman caught it, but barely, and by the time he got control of the ball, his throw to second for the double play was pitifully late.

"Got him," Zamboni said.

"You got the guy on third," Josh said, "maybe."

"No, that would've gotten him."

"Maybe," Josh said, "but, can I show you something?"

"Like what?"

"You're the one that asked me," Josh said.

"Okay," Zamboni said. "Tell me."

Josh glanced at Coach Q, who was cheerfully hitting a pop fly to the first baseman.

"After you get a handle on the ball," Josh said, "if you're that close? You just toss it underhand to first."

"Toss it?"

"Like a beanbag." Josh paused to snatch up a grounder from Coach Q, tossing it underhand to the third baseman, who grabbed it bare-handed and then rifled it to second.

"See?" Josh said, looking back at Zamboni. "Just a toss. Makes it easy for him to catch. He can even grab it without his glove. He snatches it and fires off the throw if there's a double-play opportunity."

"It takes longer to toss it," Zamboni said.

"Right. But if you're that close, it doesn't matter. Trust me."

"Zamboni!" Coach Q shouted. "Move it back. You're too close."

"You got it, Coach," Zamboni said in a goofy voice before he jogged deeper into left.

After warm-ups, the team jogged to the dugout and lined up for "The Star-Spangled Banner." Coach Q gave them a pep talk and sent them back out onto the field.

"Time for the playmakers to do their thing," Benji said loudly as he clapped Josh on the back.

"Playmakers?" Josh said.

Benji looked at him as if in shock. "What? You don't know that's our nickname? You and me, *the playmakers*."

"Who gave us that nickname?" Josh asked.

Benji looked insulted as he patted his own chest. "Me. Who else?"

Josh just shook his head and laughed as he jogged to his spot in the infield.

The first Lowville batter stepped up and Camren Fries went to work. The top of the Lowville order sprayed the field with well-hit balls, and it wasn't until Josh made a diving grab for a line drive, then fired the ball from a sitting position on the grass to second for a double play, that the inning ended.

As they entered the dugout, Camren found Josh and put a hand on his shoulder.

"What's going on?" Camren asked. "These guys are smacking every curveball I throw. It's not working. Did you watch me? What should I do?"

Josh stole a quick glance at Coach Q, then leaned toward Camren's ear and said, "I was watching your windup, and you're tipping your curveball."

"Tipping it?"

"I wasn't sure until that last hit," Josh said, "but I saw it, and the batter did, too. I think they know when your curveball is coming because you're looking at the laces of the ball before your windup."

"Looking at the laces?" Camren said.

"Yeah." Josh showed him. "Like this. Every other pitch, you just adjust the laces behind your back, but a curveball, you look at it. So, all you got to do is stop. You think you can?"

"Why not?" Camren asked.

"Well, it's a habit," Josh said. "It's harder than you think, but you can do it. Now you know about it, you'll be able to."

Camren grinned hard at Josh and said, "Thanks, Coach."

"You need something, Camren?" Coach Q asked, and Josh spun around.

CHAPTER TWENTY

"NO, COACH," CAMREN SAID. "I was just telling Josh that we're lucky we got such a good coach."

"Thanks, Camren," Coach Q said before turning away to consult his BlackBerry.

Camren just winked at Josh. The next inning, when he took the mound, Camren glanced over at Josh and gave him a thumbs-up. Josh returned the sign and Camren fiddled with the ball behind his back, finding the laces without looking at them, then going into his windup and delivering a wicked curveball.

"Strike!" the umpire cried as the batter swung and missed by a mile.

Josh and Camren grinned at each other, and then Camren picked the batters apart.

The Lowville pitcher was no slouch either, though, and the game was tied going into the last inning. When

Josh stepped up to the plate with just one out and a man on first, he half expected the pitcher to intentionally walk him. But, unlike in the first game, this pitcher wasn't going to run from Josh no matter what. Josh gave him what, smacking it over the fence and driving in the runner on first before crossing the plate himself and taking a two-run lead into the bottom of the sixth. Despite a Lowville home run to bring the score to within one, Camren finished strong, pitching the entire game and giving Lyncourt their second win.

When the team rushed Camren and raised him up on their shoulders, Camren pointed at Josh and said, "We ought to be carrying *him*."

Josh hung his head and faded away as the other kids greeted their parents. Josh watched as moms kissed their sons' cheeks and dads messed up their hair. He felt a sharp pang of regret that his own parents weren't at the game to see him. But, instead of feeling sorry for himself, Josh remembered that if he did make it to the pros one day, it would be a lonely life on the road, so he might as well get used to it now. Thinking of his situation as training for his future success put a smile on Josh's face.

Yet, even though he felt like things were coming together brilliantly with the Lyncourt team, Josh's smile couldn't survive the conversation he'd have later on, back at the hotel, with his mom.

CHAPTER TWENTY-ONE

SHE DIDN'T TALK ABOUT her troubles, but Josh sensed a strain and weariness in his mom's voice that screamed to him of her pain. His father had trained him well, though, and even though he was only twelve, Josh considered himself a baseball player. He knew he had to disregard the outside world if he wanted to be great. And now, more than ever before, Josh wanted to be great. He felt that if one thing could mend the broken pieces of his life, playing in the World Series was it.

As far as his dad went, Josh knew he would have been there if he hadn't had to coach the Titans in a tournament in Philadelphia. On the phone, his dad sounded upbeat and, without knowing it, he let Josh know he was on the right track by encouraging him to keep doing his best.

"A champion always plays like a champion," his father said. "No distractions. Just focus."

Josh did just that—he played like a champion. The next day, against a tough Schenectady team, as Josh rounded the bases after hitting a home run that brought two other runners home to win the game, he so thoroughly forgot his troubles that he looked up into the stands, expecting to see his dad's and mom's smiling faces. Not seeing them pricked his heart, but the pain quickly went away. There were other smiling faces: his teammates'. As Josh and his fellow all-stars changed from a bunch of players into a real team, working together, the magical effect it had on Josh became more and more powerful.

Even in the periods of slowest action—like the round Niko Fedchenko pitched a two-hitter against Little Falls and Josh only touched a live ball once all game with his glove—Josh still lost himself in the sunshine, the grass and dirt, the anticipation, the banter, and the action of his teammates as they battled toward another win. On the field, playing and winning ball games, it was easy to pretend that life was grand.

Zamboni was a perfect example. When they were in the dugout or on the field, Zamboni would sometimes smile at Josh and Josh would offer words of encouragement. Off the field, though, around the hotel and even on the team bus, Zamboni would sometimes whisper to one of the other players and chuckle, with his eyes flickering Josh's way. In return, when Josh encountered Zamboni in a hallway or at meals, he would look away without a word, pretending Zamboni didn't exist.

One thing Josh couldn't pretend away was his frustration with Coach Q's lack of baseball knowledge. But, instead of complaining to his father when they spoke on the phone, Josh kept the coaching he did with his teammates to himself, even though he was proud of the way it seemed to be helping them win game after game. In five games he personally hit seven home runs with only two strikeouts. Word of his prowess quickly spread through the tournament so that people stared and pointed at him, whispering to each other that he'd been the standout player leading a travel team to the national championship at Cooperstown and had been interviewed on HBO with Bob Costas about his rivalry with the son of Mickey Mullen, one of the all-time greats in the game.

Josh kept his head down around the stadium and at the hotel, avoiding eye contact with strangers and sticking mostly to his room, where he could read and relax.

In the end, they won it all, qualifying for the right to move on to the state finals. Josh and his team cheered their way down the thruway, all 150 miles, pausing only for slices of pizza at a rest stop. They talked excitedly about playing in the state finals out on Long Island and even dared to dream about winning the Mid-Atlantic Regional tournament in New Jersey the week after that. They soon reached the Grant Middle School parking lot, where a small crowd of parents and supporters greeted them with banners, streamers, and wild cheering. Josh pressed his face to the window. Nowhere did he see his mom, even though she'd told him the night before that she'd be there to pick him up.

The bus stopped and Josh hurried off, still scanning the faces, ignoring the applause, and barely feeling the congratulatory slaps on his back. He pushed through the crowd. Suddenly it parted, and he knew in his gut why his mom hadn't shown up.

CHAPTER TWENTY-TWO

"WHERE'S MY MOM?" JOSH asked, knowing that the question would make Diane squirm and pleased when it did.

Diane recovered quickly, though.

"We thought we'd have a little celebration," she said, rolling her eyes at Josh's dad. "Just you, your dad, me, and Marcus. You boys both played incredibly. It really is exciting.

"And," Diane added, with a wicked sparkle in her eye, "the two of us have a little business to take care of down in New York City, and we're going to time it so we can do that and see you boys play in the state finals at the same time. Won't that be special?"

Zamboni shoved himself rudely into their midst and swung an arm around his mom's waist, giving her half a hug. Josh's dad held out a hand, offering to slap Zamboni five.

"Congratulations, Marcus," Josh's dad said.

Marcus gave Josh's father a disgusted look and half-heartedly slapped his hand.

Josh waited for his father to grab Zamboni by the neck and shake him up for showing such disrespect, but all he did was smile and nod. Josh felt the rest-stop pizza jump up out of his stomach and into his throat. He gulped it back to keep from vomiting. Before he could come up with a reason why he couldn't go for ice cream with these people, his father spoke.

"Celebration, as in a little Friendly's ice cream," his father said, grinning stupidly at Diane. "Banana splits on me."

"Mom," Zamboni said, pouting, "you said *we* were going to do something special."

"We are," Diane said. "You and me and Josh and his father are going for ice cream."

"Oh, great," Zamboni said sarcastically, letting Josh know he meant the exact opposite. "That's really special."

"Oh, come on, Marcus," Josh's dad said. "It'll be fun."

Without even looking to see Josh's reaction, his father turned and led them all to the parking lot, where he put on a pair of sunglasses and got in behind the wheel of Diane's Audi convertible. He popped the trunk open and both Josh and Zamboni dumped their bags in. Diane opened the passenger side and tilted her seat forward. Zamboni climbed in behind Josh's dad and slumped in the corner.

Josh hesitated.

He felt that if he got in, he was somehow committing himself to something bigger than ice cream, and that thing made him sick, everything about it. Diane with her bright red purse, skintight jeans, and high-heeled shoes. Zamboni, with his reluctant appreciation for Josh's knowledge and skill. Josh's feet told him to just run. Run across the parking lot, down Grant Avenue, and into his own neighborhood, where his mother was probably waiting for him, sitting at the kitchen table crying her eyes out.

His heart told him no. Despite his mom, despite the fear he often felt of his father, even sitting there with those stupid sunglasses on his face, Josh's father owned his heart. Josh didn't think he could ever walk away from the man.

He got in and let Diane bang the seat back into his knees. Zamboni dug in his ear for wax. Josh's dad downshifted the Audi and raced out of the lot with a boyish grin. Josh leaned back and closed his eyes, letting the warm wind whip past his face and thinking back to the bad things he must have done to deserve such a disastrous turn of events.

CHAPTER TWENTY-THREE

JOSH PUSHED THE BANANA around into the melted swirl of ice cream, pineapple sauce, and hot fudge so that it looked like he'd eaten a little bit. He was too focused on trying to keep down the pizza that was already in his stomach, though, and not about to add anything new to the mix. His father and Diane actually giggled. That was the killer. She dabbed a bit of whipped cream on the end of his nose and his father—all six foot six, two hundred and eighty-three pounds of him—giggled.

Josh saw Zamboni looking, too, and the hateful glare he cast upon Josh's dad. Josh looked away, pretending to be interested in a blue parrot tattoo wrapped around the waitress's calf as she presented the check to the table across the aisle. When the waitress collected her money, it made Josh think of something Diane had said that he'd been meaning to ask his father about. It would be a good distraction from their giggling anyway.

"Dad," Josh said, "what kind of business do you have going on down in New York City?"

Josh's dad and Diane smiled at each other. His dad sat up a bit straighter, cleared his throat, and said, "Some potential financial deals, with a bank, maybe."

"Financial deals?" Josh asked.

"It's complicated," his dad said, glancing at Diane, who looked up at him with worship in her eyes. "Sometimes, when you have a contract like my Nike deal, investment banks will do what they call a 'monetization.'"

Josh couldn't help looking confused.

"They basically assign a value to your contract and give you the money up front," Josh's dad said. "It's kind of complicated."

"Yeah, that's what you said," Josh said, scratching the back of his neck.

"Having all the money up front allows you to borrow even more and do deals that make you real money, big money," his father said.

"What do the banks get out of it?" Josh asked.

"Well, you pay them a premium for giving you the money up front. They have to wait to collect the money from the contract, but they get some extra. Not too much, but that's what banks do. This is how people create wealth, Josh. It's a different mind-set than most of the people you've been exposed to have."

His father's voice oozed with excitement. "Most people just try to get by, make enough money to pay the bills like I was doing. To create wealth, you have to monetize and you have to leverage. Trust me, when I buy you one of those new Camaros for your sixteenth birthday, you'll thank me."

When Josh's dad and Diane smiled at each other, Josh leaned toward Zamboni and in a whisper said, "Hear that, Zamboni? A Camaro? What'll you drive? A Hyundai?"

Before Josh could say anything else, Zamboni—who sat on the inside of the booth next to Josh—scooted himself over so that his butt was halfway onto Josh's leg before he squeaked out a fart. Josh squirmed away, scowling. Zamboni acted as if nothing had happened, but after another minute, he scooted closer again.

"Hey," Josh said, turning on Zamboni with a raised fist. "Cut the crap. You want to get out to use the bathroom or something? Just ask."

Zamboni gave Josh a look of surprise, as if he had no idea what had happened.

"Josh!" his dad said. "What's wrong with you?"

"This creep's scooting his butt over on my leg and farting is what," Josh said, springing out of his seat and shoving Zamboni, who fell back more than he had to and bumped his head into the wall.

"Real nice," Diane said in a mutter Josh could barely hear.

"Here," Zamboni said, rubbing the back of his head

and patting the seat, "there's plenty of room. I didn't mean to crowd you. There's something sticky on the seat over here is all."

Josh's dad's face went red. He stood up and said, "Let's go."

"Dad," Josh said, but his father slapped thirty dollars onto the table and started to walk out.

Diane murmured something soothing into his father's ear and Zamboni slouched along behind. When he hit the parking lot, Josh thought about running. But the thing about him running away was that either his father would catch him or, worse, he might not even try. Josh climbed into the backseat and hung his head. He didn't look up until they pulled in front of his house. Diane got out and tilted the seat forward so he could leave.

"See you," Josh said in Zamboni's direction with a half wave.

Josh got out and retrieved his bags from the trunk. He stood next to Diane at the curb, weighed down by his things. His father's car stood in the driveway, so Josh looked expectantly at his dad, thinking they'd finally have a chance to be alone together.

"Great job in Albany, Josh," Zamboni said in a cheerful tone Josh knew was meant to impress the adults.

"Uh, thanks," Josh said, glancing at Zamboni before his eyes returned to his dad, who only stared out toward the end of the street. "You, too."

"That's better," Diane said, patting Josh on the head

as if he were three years old. "We should all get along, don't you think?"

Josh couldn't help squirming out of her reach and retreating to the sidewalk before he turned and said, "Dad? You coming?"

Without looking at him, Josh's father said, "You go. Your mom will want to see you. We'll talk."

Diane climbed in and flickered her fingers at Josh. The car pulled away. Josh watched them go, shielding his eyes from the sun. Zamboni spun around in the backseat, made a stupid face, and thumbed his nose at Josh.

Shaking his head, Josh trudged up the driveway under the weight of his duffel and bat bags. He set the bat bag down in a corner of the garage, wondering what it meant that his father left the silver Taurus there. Without the car, his dad had no way to get to work. Josh crossed the driveway to the kitchen door on the side of the house. The metal frame of the broken screen door screeched as he opened it, and the wooden door leading inside groaned.

Josh dumped the duffel bag on the floor and shouted, "I'm home!"

He entered the kitchen to see his mom sitting in the corner at the table. Her eyes were puffy and red, but when she saw Josh, she jumped up and smoothed her dress and headed for the sink.

"Sit down," she said, her back to him and her hands

busy with the clatter of dishes in the sink. "I'll fix you something."

"We had pizza on the way," Josh said, looking around for a sign of his little sister. "Mom? What's wrong?"

His mother stiffened.

"He didn't tell you, did he?" his mom asked, her hands gripping the edge of the sink.

"Who didn't tell me what?" Josh asked.

CHAPTER TWENTY-FOUR

"HE'S MOVING IN WITH her," Josh's mother said.

Josh felt for the back of the nearest chair to steady himself.

"Gran is here to help," his mom said, her voice unnaturally soft. "She took Laurel to the park. He did pick you up, didn't he? You didn't have to walk home?"

"No," Josh said, slumping into the seat and feeling sick at the news. "He told me he was getting an apartment."

"At least he did one thing he said he would," she said. "He picked you up." His mother turned to face him, her hands twisting a dish towel.

"What's it mean?" Josh asked.

His mother's face crumpled with agony. "It means he's not coming back. Not ever. He's with her now."

"He took me for ice cream with her," Josh said,

almost to himself.

"He didn't even have the guts to tell you." Bitterness crept into her voice.

"I hate him."

"Josh, you shouldn't say that." His mom looked like she'd been hit with a board.

Josh jumped up out of the chair. He gripped two handfuls of his hair as he sprinted through the living room and bounded up the stairs.

"I hate him!" Josh screamed, and he slammed his bedroom door shut and locked it.

The room spun. Josh knocked the books off the top of his dresser, scattering them across the floor along with his two granite bookends. He threw himself on the bed and screamed into his pillow, pressing it around his head to mute the world. He heard his mom knock softly at the bedroom door, but after a while she went away. Josh rolled onto his back to study a crack in a ceiling that sloped with the roofline right down to the head of his bed. When the cell phone in his pocket vibrated, he snapped it open, hoping the text was from his father so he could fire off some nasty response.

It was Jaden, asking if he wanted to hang out.

"No," he texted back.

After a few seconds she texted again to ask what was wrong.

"Everything," he texted.

The phone rang and he picked it up.

"You just made it to the state finals," Jaden said.

"What do you mean, 'everything'?"

"I don't want to talk about it."

Jaden huffed into the phone. "Do I have to come over there?"

"You can do what you want," Josh said.

"I always do." Then she hung up.

Josh wasn't quite sure what she'd do, but he wasn't surprised—and he had to admit he also wasn't disappointed—when he heard the doorbell ring and then Jaden's footsteps climbing the stairs. She knocked. He let her in and wandered back to his bed. She sat beside him on its edge and put a hand on his back.

"I'm sorry," she said.

"You don't even know what this is about."

"I saw your mom's eyes," she said. "I know."

"I hate him," Josh said, his eyes swimming in tears even as he looked at his friend.

She nodded but wore an almost hurt expression. "You don't have to do that, though. Your mom's not like that."

"I hate him for me," Josh said. "You can't even imagine what all this feels like, Jaden. It's like nothing ever hurt before. Even when that jerk threw a beanball at me and cracked my eye socket. I wish I could have that happen ten times over again instead of this. You can't even imagine it."

Jaden looked down at her hands. Her chin slumped to her chest.

"No, you're wrong," she said. "I can't say exactly, but I can imagine. You forget about my mom. I never saw her, never knew her. When I do something good, or if I wear something pretty, people will say, 'I bet your mother is so proud,' and it hurts all over like she just died, every time."

"I'm sorry," Josh said, meaning it.

"That's okay," she said, looking over at him. "But you've got to admit that half your dad is better than no dad. Look how many people's parents are divorced. Look at Benji. Over half the marriages in this country end in divorce. It's nothing new."

"But *not* having your mom," Josh said, "that's got to make you know how bad I want to have my dad since he's *here*. Imagine what you'd do if you could get her back. I'm sorry; I didn't mean it like that."

"It's okay," Jaden said. "I know what you mean. I'll help you if I can."

She knelt down on the floor and began to pick up the books Josh had knocked off his dresser, scooping them up into the crook of her arm.

"To have to share him with that total idiot, Zamboni?" Josh said, shaking his head. "I don't know if I can do it. I really don't. I hate that kid—and his mom and my dad. It's like they're after this one big happy baseball family thing. First she puts me with him instead of Benji to room on the road, then we have this stupid little ice-cream celebration. I swear, I almost vomited today just being with them all in the same place. I mean, literally vomited, not just the expression."

"I'm not siding with him or anything," Jaden said, picking the granite bookends up off the floor and setting the books back up on the dresser. "You know that, right? But think about his deal. He's got the same thing you do, a mom and dad who are split. I bet he doesn't like it any more than you do."

"Yeah, well my parents weren't split until that tramp mother of his went after my dad," Josh said.

"Well," Jaden said, sandwiching the books between the hunks of granite to hold them upright, "I'm just saying. For him, it probably seems just as bad."

"The guy is a royal pain," Josh said. "He flicks his boogers around like spitballs. He's as stupid as his name. Did I tell you he smokes cigarettes when no one's around? I doubt he'd even be on the team if his mom wasn't the league secretary. That's probably why she does it."

"When things are bad like this," Jaden said, turning one of the bookends from the rough rocky surface so that the shiny polished part faced out, "you've got to try and look for the bright side. There's always a bright side. Well, almost always."

"Right," Josh said, "*almost* always, but not in this case. There is nothing good about this, and nothing good about that woman and her stupid son. Well, unless you count her doctoring the books so Benji could play on the all-star team."

"What do you mean?" Jaden asked, wrinkling her forehead.

Josh told her the story about Benji not being at the game on Memorial Day, but his name being mysteriously logged into the record book, then he said, "So, yeah, I guess she has one redeeming quality—she used her spectacular ability to cheat and lie to get Benji on my team so that I'd go to Albany and she could pull a vampire move on my dad. So I guess you're right, Jaden. There is a bright side."

"You don't have to sound so bitter, Josh," Jaden said, removing her hand from the bookend. "I'm just trying to help, but you know, you're right: this *is* a bright side."

"I was being sarcastic," Josh said.

"A person who cheats like that doesn't do it just once," Jaden said.

"I'm sure you're right about that," Josh said. "She's rotten to the core."

"And if she is," Jaden said slowly, "I know how to fix her good."

Josh felt his heart pick up its pace at the thought of sinking Diane's ship. It was almost too good to be true.

But Josh knew how smart Jaden was, so he asked, "How?"

CHAPTER TWENTY-FIVE

"SOMETIMES," JADEN SAID, "WHEN people first meet, everything seems great, like they can do no wrong. They call it lovesick. Your dad's lovesick. But, the good news is that once you break that spell, it's over for good. All it takes is just one cold hard fact, one thing to prove to the lovesick person how wrong they are, and they're free."

"What cold hard fact?" Josh asked.

"I'm not sure," Jaden said, "but it'll be my job to find out."

"And you think you could do that for me?" Josh asked. He knew that besides being smart, Jaden's dream was to one day win a Pulitzer Prize for her writing as an investigative journalist. He'd seen firsthand how talented she was when it came to snooping out information about people, and he had no doubts she'd one day win her prize. Meantime, her investigating skills just might help mend the gaping hole in his life.

"Who knows?" she said. "I'll do my best."

"I mean," Josh said, getting excited, "what kind of things do you think she could have done?"

Jaden shrugged. "Who knows? People lie, they cheat, steal, do drugs."

"You think she does drugs?" Josh said hopefully. "My dad would never go for that."

"I don't think anything," Jaden said. "People do things that are wrong. Usually the ones who do one thing wrong have got a whole closet full of them they keep hidden. That's human nature. That's why we have police and judges and jails."

"How long will it take you?" Josh asked.

"It doesn't happen overnight," Jaden said.

"Weeks?"

"Maybe," she said. "I'll do my best."

"Because I don't want him getting too far along with her," Josh said.

"They didn't tell you that they're getting married or anything?" Jaden said.

"No," Josh said. "Not that I know of. How could they? They just met."

Jaden looked at him.

Josh said, "You're making me nervous."

CHAPTER TWENTY-SIX

JOSH ONLY HAD TWO days before he had to leave with the team for the state finals out on Long Island. He stayed busy getting all his lawns cut and reading a scary book called *The Lurker at the Threshold* by H. P. Lovecraft. One afternoon he, Jaden, and Benji went to Oneida Shores with Benji's mom to swim, lie out in the sun, and eat hot dogs cooked on one of the park's small braziers set in concrete next to the picnic tables.

Josh tried to avoid being home, mainly because he couldn't stop feeling the emptiness created by his father's absence. He was beginning to wonder if he'd ever even see his father again when he called Josh the night before the team left for Long Island.

"How you doing?" his father asked.

"Fine," Josh said, searching for words that could

capture everything he felt and knowing they didn't exist.

"Good," his father said. "So, I wanted to check to see where your head is at before I extend this business trip down to New York City to include your games."

"What do you mean my head?"

"I mean, are you going to act mature about everything?" his father said. "Or are you going to push Marcus around and make me look like a bad father?"

Josh wanted to tell his father that he didn't need anyone's help to look like a bad father. The words were right on his tongue, but they wouldn't come out. No matter how mad Josh was, and even with his father miles away, the notion of back-talking his father made Josh move the phone away from his face for a moment. He'd grown up thinking of his father as the giant in the story "Jack and the Beanstalk," dark and brooding and frighteningly large, with a booming voice.

"I'm going to act mature," Josh said softly.

"So, you want me to see you play?" his father asked. "The Titans don't have a tournament until the following week and I'll be down there anyway meeting with the banks, but I'm not going out to Long Island unless you're on board."

"I'm on board."

"With everything?" his dad asked. "Diane? Marcus?"

"Yes, Dad," Josh said. "I'm on board with everything."

When he hung up, Josh texted Jaden, asking her

how the investigation was coming. Jaden replied that she didn't have anything so far. Josh snapped his phone shut and packed for the tournament.

Downstairs, what was left of his family was waiting for him at the dinner table.

"Sorry," Josh said. "I was packing."

"I wish you'd get that lawn cut," Gran said, peering out the window. "And these windows cleaned. Lots to do without a man around the house now."

Josh's mom looked down and cleared her throat. "Josh has baseball, Mom."

"Baseball, baseball," Gran said with an angry glint in her eyes. "That silly game has done enough damage already. With everything going on, Laura, I still think Josh should stick around here to help you rather than running around the world playing that game."

Josh already felt guilty, sensing that his baseball wins and the Nike deal had caused all the problems in the first place. So Gran's remark cut him deep. But rather than arguing about her words or denying their truth, he found it easier just to stay quiet.

"Mom," Josh's mom said, folding her hands. "Please don't start. Let me say grace."

As Josh's mom thanked God for everything they had, Josh couldn't help from wondering how she could be so upbeat with his dad being gone, but he kept his mouth closed tight like his eyes. When he opened his eyes, Gran had him in her sights again. He sighed and reached for the mashed potatoes, spooning out a small mountain before dousing them with gravy, string beans, and slices of chicken. While Josh ate, Gran pushed food around on her plate as if trying to achieve some kind of order to it all.

"It's just that there are things that need to be done around here," she said with a sniff. "Josh is going to have to be the man of the family. Games need to come second."

"Josh is good at baseball, Mom," Josh's mom said, looking at him proudly. "I want him to go."

"Good at baseball?" Gran said. "What does that *mean*?"

"That I've got what it takes to go pro one day," Josh said, his cheeks warming at the boldness of his own statement.

"Pro," Gran said as if it were some kind of toilet talk. "That's nothing to aspire to if you ask me. Your father was a 'pro.'"

"He made a living for thirteen years," Josh said, casually filling his mouth with food and chewing slow.

Gran rolled her eyes around the kitchen, coming to rest on the big water stain over the refrigerator.

"Not much of a living if you ask me," Gran said, staring at the stain.

"Oh, Mom!" Josh's mom said, tossing down her napkin and leaving the table with tears in her eyes. "You're not helping."

Josh heard her footsteps on the stairs and a sob that sounded like it escaped from both hands covering her face.

CHAPTER TWENTY-SEVEN

LAUREL GAVE A PUZZLED look and called for her mommy to come back. Then she started to cry.

"Oh, fiddlesticks," Gran said, groaning as she rose and scooped Laurel out of her seat before cooing softly into her ear and walking off into the living room.

Josh shook his head and plowed through his meal. It was the kind of drama that made him actually look forward to Long Island. If he could only figure out how to ditch Zamboni and get Benji back as his roommate, the whole thing would be awesome, but that couldn't happen. He'd promised his father that he'd be "on board." You didn't promise Josh's dad something and then not do it, no matter how mad you might be at him—you just didn't. Besides, Coach Q had made it pretty clear that he didn't want Josh asking for a roommate change again.

Josh cleaned his plate, then washed it along with his silverware and glass in the sink before going to his room. Gran was rocking Laurel in the TV room, and Josh could hear his mom's soft crying as he passed her bedroom door. He stopped and pressed his face and hands against the door's smooth surface, aching for her to stop but finally realizing she wouldn't.

He brushed his teeth and washed up, then tiptoed into his bedroom, where he buried his head in the pillows, holding them tight to block out all sound. Sleep dodged him for a long time. He tossed and turned, sweating in the jungle of sheets before exhaustion finally took him down deep, beneath even the place of dreams, so that when he awoke the next morning he had to wonder if he'd slept at all.

In the morning Josh's mom made him French toast and tried to be cheerful, but she couldn't hide the puffy skin around her red eyes and the flat tone of her voice. Gran's words about Josh sticking around the house to help out haunted him as he rode alongside his mom on the way to Grant Middle, but they also made him even more eager to get back to baseball.

"Don't worry," she said, patting his leg as they pulled up behind the bus, "I'll be all right."

He kissed his mom, glancing only briefly into her sad eyes, said good-bye, and hurried across the parking lot.

The charter bus sat puking up diesel fumes, and

even on board the bus, enough of the fumes leaked in to turn everyone's skin a pale shade of green. Coach Q wandered onto the bus with a super-size cup of coffee and a tangle of bed-head hair way beneath the dignity of a championship coach. Still, he had the power to circle his index finger, pretend to tug on a train whistle, and set the big bus into motion as if he'd really pulled the engine's levers. The trip to Long Island took nearly seven hours, but thankfully Josh got to sit with Benji while Zamboni sat in the back corner of the bus bobbling his head to whatever crazy tunes he had on his iPod.

When they got to the Holiday Inn Express, Josh crossed his fingers and picked his key up off the table: 207. He found Benji's envelope with his eyes and saw 219. There was still hope, though. Maybe Coach Q had put him with another player—anyone but Zamboni. Before Josh could find Zamboni's envelope, the mop-headed boy snatched it off the table so Josh couldn't get a look. Zamboni's iPod earphones were cranked up so loud, Josh could hear his music. Zamboni checked the number and grinned at Josh before marching off with his head bouncing to the beat.

It was faster for Josh to climb the stairs instead of waiting to jam himself into the elevator with the rest of the guys. He unlocked his room and left it open since he could see Zamboni bopping his head as he walked down the hall from the elevators. Josh put his stuff down and collapsed on the bed. When he heard Zamboni's music pass by, Josh's heart picked up its pace and he shot up off the bed.

He peeked out the doorway. Zamboni kept going down the hall, music playing. Josh turned. Callan Fries approached, fumbling with his key. Josh grinned wide at him but stopped when Callan opened the door across the hall.

"Boo!"

Josh jumped and spun. Zamboni had turned off his music and snuck up behind Josh to scare him. Zamboni laughed hysterically.

"You should see your face," Zamboni said between gasps for air. "That scar lights up like a neon sign."

"Great," Josh said, his heart weighted with hatred and sinking fast. "You're hilarious."

"I hear that." Zamboni glided past him and dumped his stuff in the room. "The three H's: hilarious, handsome, and heavenly."

"You've been listening to your mom too much," Josh said, passing him by and digging into his bag to unpack his clothes for the week. After a minute of silence, Josh turned to find Zamboni standing right behind him with fists clenched.

"You don't say anything about my mom," Zamboni said through clenched teeth, his eyes swirling with insanity. "You got that?"

Josh swallowed. He was taller and bigger than

Zamboni, but he sensed a wildness that he wasn't certain he could match.

"Sure," Josh said.

"Because I never said a word about *your* mom."

Josh studied Zamboni's face, his own hands curling into fists. If this mope said a word about his mom, he'd tear him to pieces. The thought of his mom crying to herself because of Zamboni's own mother lit a reckless fire deep inside him.

"And you better not," Josh said. "Because she's not some tramp, like yours."

Before Josh could react, Zamboni's fist crashed into the side of his face.

Josh saw stars.

CHAPTER TWENTY-EIGHT

JOSH KNEW HE WAS on the floor and he felt something thumping his ribs. Up and down the thumping went. As Josh's head cleared from the punch, he heard shouting and realized that Zamboni was jumping up and down on top of him like an ape at the zoo. Callan knocked Zamboni off. Josh staggered up and fired a punch at Zamboni's jaw. Zamboni's head snapped back. Benji piled into the room and yanked Josh backward before pushing Zamboni into the window to separate them. Josh tripped and fell to the floor. Coach Q appeared, bellowing like a wounded lion.

Josh found his feet and got back up. Zamboni struggled against Callan and Benji, still trying to get at Josh. Coach Q stepped in and grabbed two fistfuls of Zamboni's shirt.

"Stop!" the coach hollered. "Right now!"

Even Zamboni reacted to the earsplitting roar.

"Now," Coach Q said, huffing, "you two cut it out. No more. LeBlanc, get your things. You're moving. Vito?

"Vito!"

"I'm here, Dad," Vito Quatropanni said, slipping into the hotel room past the crowd of Lyncourt players.

"You get your stuff and move in with Marcus," Coach Q said. "Josh, you get out. Benji, get his things and take them to your room. It's disgusting. Two teammates can't even get along. How are we gonna win this thing?"

Every fiber in Josh's body ached to scream at Coach Q, to tell him the whole thing was *his* fault. Josh hated Zamboni, and if Coach Q had a crumb of sense he'd have known to keep them apart. Josh had *asked* to be with Benji. He hated Coach Q and added him to the growing list. Only his father's strict discipline kept Josh from screaming. He bit his lower lip and marched out, his face hot with shame.

Josh started down the hallway toward Benji's room. Benji caught up with him just as Vito came out of the room carrying his stuff and offering a nasty look to Josh as they swapped room keys. Vito headed silently for Zamboni's room like a boy being sent off to prison.

Benji looked sadly after Vito, removed the room key from his pocket, and said, "Man, poor Vito."

"Poor Vito?"

"He's got a very weak stomach," Benji said, swinging open the door so Josh could push past him into the room. "I hope he can handle Zamboni's humor."

"What about me?" Josh asked.

"Dude," Benji said, "I'm glad we're roomies again, don't get me wrong. I'm just saying, you gotta deal with Zamboni anyway. He's practically your brother. Vito's just an innocent bystander."

"He is *not* practically my brother!" Josh said, his hands curling into fists again.

Benji looked at Josh's hands, then into his eyes and said, "Dude, you need anger management."

"Thanks, Benji," Josh said, dropping his things and throwing himself down on the bed.

"My mom always tells my dad that the first thing you gotta do with a problem is admit you have it," Benji said. "That's all I'm saying."

"The problem isn't me," Josh said.

"Look, I don't mean to be insensitive," Benji said, "but your parents splitting up isn't the end of the world. Look at me. There are advantages."

Josh looked over and saw that Benji was serious.

"Like *what*?" he asked.

Benji scratched behind one ear and said, "Dude, you can play one off against the other and pretty much get anything you want. Like, let's say you want to stay up on a school night because Selena Gomez is going to be on *The Late Show*."

"I don't care about Selena Gomez on *The Late Show,*" Josh said.

"That's another issue altogether, Josh," Benji said. "Work with me here. You want to stay up late and your mom says 'No, it's a school night.' So what do you do? You say, 'Dad lets me stay up late at his house if there's something special on.' Bingo, your mom caves like a sand castle at high tide. The advantages are endless: homework, birthday presents, sleepovers, you name it. A kid with divorced parents lives in a universe of untold freedom. So, relax."

"I don't care about that stuff," Josh said. "I want my family the way it was."

Benji tilted his head. "That's the shock talking. Everyone goes into shock initially. Once you're over it, you realize it's like a swine flu shot. Stings a bit, but not a huge deal in the big picture, and the benefits are long-term."

Josh pulled a pillow over his head.

Josh could hear Benji whistling and banging the drawers as he unpacked his belongings. Then things went quiet for a bit. Josh removed the pillow. Benji stood over him with his arms crossed.

"Dude," Benji said, "I know it hurts, but get over it. Come on. Let's go eat dinner and then Callan's got some horror movies and I've got my dad's laptop to play them on."

"How the heck did you get your dad to give you his

laptop for the week?" Josh asked.

"Have you been listening to me?" Benji asked. "Listen and learn. Come on. Let's eat and watch movies. Don't lie here and pout. You could use a good distraction. Then, tomorrow, we got some baseball to play."

"My dad's coming the day after tomorrow with that bimbo," Josh said.

"Come on, Josh."

"He's going to kill me," Josh said, touching the tender part of his face where Zamboni had clocked him. "I promised I'd get 'on board.' That's what he called it. Pathetic."

"He doesn't have to know," Benji said.

"Right. You think he's not going to find out?" Josh said, squinting at Benji. "I bet Zamboni tells that mother everything. My dad will know, and I don't even want to think about what he'll say."

"Think positive. Everyone else is going to be talking about how great we played to advance to the next round. Your dad won't know if Zamboni doesn't tell him."

"How could that ever happen?" Josh asked.

Benji smiled and said, "Leave it to me."

CHAPTER TWENTY-NINE

BENJI WENT TO THE dresser and removed his father's laptop from the duffel bag, opening it up on the desk.

"I'll Skype him," Benji said, booting up the computer.

"Benji, you're not making any sense," Josh said, sitting up to watch. "What do you mean you'll Skype him?"

"You know what Skype is?"

"Sure," Josh said. "The computer thing where you can see them talking to you on your screen and they can see you on theirs? What's that got to do with this?"

"Blackmail," Benji said, typing furiously, then pausing to take out his cell phone and send a quick text.

"What? Who?" Josh asked.

"Zamboni, that's who," Benji said, spinning the desk chair so that he looked at Josh as he held up his phone.

"I just texted Vito. He's got Skype, and he brought his laptop with him, too."

"Vito has a laptop?"

"Josh, Coach Q is a Mercedes salesman."

"Oh."

Benji's phone vibrated. He checked the incoming message and said, "So, Vito's in the game. I asked him to boot up and throw the Skype on and to just leave the camera on a wide angle but black out his own screen while we go eat dinner. I told him not to tell Zamboni."

"Benji, you're still not making sense."

"Don't you get it?" Benji said. "You're the one who kept complaining last week that Zamboni was smoking in the room when you weren't around. Well, we Skype him. I set my computer up to record it all. We get Vito, go to dinner, Zamboni lights up, we come back, and we got him! Skyped!"

Josh went over the plan in his mind, searching for pitfalls but finding none.

"Wow," he said. "Benji, it just might work."

"Of course it will work," Benji said, typing in a couple more things and revealing a screen that showed Zamboni sitting on his bed cutting his toenails as he watched Vito with a sullen look.

"Benji," Josh said, his mouth falling open, "I gotta hand it to you. This could really work."

CHAPTER THIRTY

"**WHEN HAVE I HAD** a plan that didn't work?" Benji asked, rising from the desk and tugging on his newest Red Sox cap. "Come on. Let's go eat dinner."

"Shouldn't we watch?" Josh asked.

"Who wants to watch some guy cut his disgusting toenails?" Benji said, glancing back at the screen. "I got it all on tape, and I'm hungry."

They left the room and started down the hallway. Josh couldn't resist sniffing at the doorway to his old room, eager for the disgusting smell of cigarette smoke. He had a hard time enjoying his dinner, even though Coach Q had a dozen boxes of pizzas lined up for them buffet-style. The team sat around a big conference table in a room meant for meetings, eating pizza and drinking sodas. Josh had just finished his third piece when

Zamboni slipped inside the meeting room, unnoticed by everyone else. Josh nudged Benji and angled his head toward Zamboni, who picked the last two slices of pepperoni out of a box.

"You know we got him," Benji said through a mouthful of pie.

"Let's go see," Josh said, dusting the flour off his hands and rising from the table.

"Easy," Benji said. "A man's gotta eat."

"You had four slices."

"Don't count my food, Josh," Benji said, stuffing almost half a sausage, pepper, and onion slice into his mouth. "It's rude."

Josh mangled his empty soda bottle so that the plastic crunched beneath his hands. Benji seemed unfazed because he went after another slice before wiping his mouth, draining his own soda, and giving Josh a wink to signal that he was ready to go. Josh couldn't help stealing a look at Zamboni, sitting off by himself and dangling a slice of pepperoni over his mouth before slurping it down.

Josh practically ran up the stairs and he snorted at Benji, who climbed at a relaxed pace, complaining that they should have taken the elevator.

"It's one floor. Come on, Benji."

Josh dashed down the hall and opened the door. He rushed to the computer and stared at the screen. It showed Zamboni's empty room. Josh went back to the door and urged Benji to hurry up.

"Dude, you've got to take it easy," Benji said, slipping into the room and sitting down at the desk.

"Did you get it?" Josh asked.

Benji turned and said, "Now, how would I know? I got to play it back."

"Well, do it."

"I'm trying."

Benji navigated through the program, typing and clicking, until the video showed Zamboni back in the room, snipping at his toenails where they'd left him. Zamboni stopped and looked up. He just sat for a while, watching Vito until Vito walked past the screen and they could hear the sound of the door closing. Zamboni looked toward the door for a minute before getting up himself and disappearing from view.

Josh heard the distinct sound of the door being locked and double locked. He and Benji looked at each other and grinned. Zamboni reappeared and flopped down on his bed. He reached into his pocket, removing a pack of cigarettes and a book of matches.

"We got him," Josh said.

But Zamboni kept digging and came up with his cell phone. He put down the cigarettes and matches and began to dial the cell phone.

"What?" Josh said. "Don't even tell me he's not going to smoke."

"Let's see," Benji said. "I wonder who he's calling."

"Dad?" Zamboni said. "Yeah, it's me. . . . No, I'm at the state finals down on Long Island. . . . Yeah. You think maybe you'll make it down here? Oh, no, I understand. That's okay, Dad. . . . Yeah, Williamsport is the big show. . . . That's right, Taiwan and teams like that, but we'll have to win this thing and then the regionals in New Jersey. *Then* we get to go to the World Series, and, yeah, that would be great if you could make it there. . . . Yeah, I know, Dad. Winners never quit and quitters never win. Thanks. Okay, well, I'll see you."

Zamboni snapped the phone shut and just sat there.

"Dude," Benji said, moving his face closer to the screen and pointing at Zamboni's face, "is that what I think it is?"

Josh watched as Zamboni scooped up the pack of cigarettes, shook one out, and lighted it.

"You got him, Benji," Josh said, relieved that they had what they needed to keep Zamboni quiet.

"I got more than that." Benji pointed at Zamboni's face. "Dude, check it out. This kid is *crying*."

CHAPTER THIRTY-ONE

JOSH COULDN'T HELP FEELING bad for Zamboni. Even after touching his own face to remind himself of the shot Zamboni had given him earlier, Josh still felt bad.

"It's time for us to tell him about *Candid Camera*," Benji said with a grin. "Man, who cares about the cigarettes? When we show him this? He'll lick the bottoms of your shoes. You won't have to worry about him blowing you in to your dad anymore."

Josh stood up and backed away. "Well, the cigarette is enough, Benji. Let's not go there with the kid crying."

"Dude, look at your face," Benji said. "It looks like you got kicked by a mule. You gotta shut him up *and* serve him."

"I don't have to serve him, Benji. We don't need to be like that."

"But you hate this guy."

"I know," Josh said, "but that doesn't matter. You just don't do that."

"He's crying like a baby."

"Because of his dad, Benji," Josh said. "You never cried about your parents splitting up? When you wanted your dad to be at something and he couldn't?"

"Me?" Benji said, sticking a thumb in his own chest. "Cry? I'm a heavy hitter, like the Babe, Reggie Jackson, like Manny Ramirez before steroids. Heavy hitters don't cry, Josh. They fight on."

Josh looked away. "I don't want that part of it, Benji."

"Well, you can't separate the two, buddy," Benji said. "He's got to see this if you want to keep him quiet."

"But I don't want you to say anything about him crying."

"What, we just act like we don't see the kid sitting there, smoking his stupid face off and crying like a total baby?"

"Right."

Benji shrugged. "Whatever."

"It doesn't require you to say anything."

"Hey," Benji said, closing up the program, "about this not requiring 'me' to say anything stuff? Who do you think is going to show him the tape, anyway?"

"Well, it's your dad's computer," Josh said. "And the whole thing was your idea."

"Yeah, to save your butt," Benji said. "*You're* the one

showing him and serving up the blackmail. I'm not doing that. It's illegal."

"Illegal?"

"I'm sure we're not going to get caught or anything," Benji said. "Even if we do, we're just kids."

"Which part of this is illegal?" Josh asked.

"Well." Benji scratched his head. "I think the taping part—I don't think you can technically do that to someone when they don't know you're doing it—and probably the blackmail part, too."

"Oh my God," Josh said, staring in horror at the computer. "Get rid of it."

"But Josh, it'll keep him quiet."

"But it's *blackmail*." Josh hushed his voice into a frantic whisper. "Of course it is. That makes sense. What was I thinking? What were you thinking?"

"Just helping you out."

"I know, but two wrongs don't make a right," Josh said. "That's basic. We should get rid of it."

"Well," Benji said, turning toward the computer, "technically, in math, if you multiply two negatives, you get a positive, so I'm not sure you're completely correct."

Josh threw up his hands. "Come on, you know what I mean. Get rid of it."

"Darn." Benji typed in some commands. "We had him."

"Did you do it?" Josh asked, looking over his shoulder.

"Yeah, you're sunk," Benji said sadly. "Your dad's gonna chew you up and spit you out."

"Yeah," Josh said, lying back on his bed. "I know."

They stayed silent for a few minutes before Benji said, "Well, you wanna watch one of those horror movies?"

"No, thanks." Josh kicked off his shoes, putting a pillow over his face and closing his eyes. "I'm going to sleep. I got a horror show of my own, right here between my ears."

Josh drifted in and out of sleep, tired but tormented by images of his father's angry scowl and his mother's puffy, bloodshot eyes. Josh knew that anyone living in a nightmare like his would give almost anything to make it go away.

When the idea came to him, he jumped up out of bed and flicked on the light. Standing over Benji, Josh shook him until he sputtered awake.

"What?" Benji said, blinking at the light. "Who?"

"Zamboni," Josh said excitedly. "Benji, I've got an idea."

CHAPTER THIRTY-TWO

"YOU'VE LOST YOUR MIND," Benji said after listening with intermittent yawns. "This time, completely."

"Why, Benji? Why won't it work?"

"Because Zamboni is an idiot," Benji said. "He's gross. He sneaks cigarettes. He called you Scarface. Come on, a guy like that? It's hopeless."

"I'm going to try, Benji," Josh said.

"Right now?" Benji said. "It's two o'clock in the morning."

"I can't sleep anyway."

"Well, the rest of us can," Benji said, lying back down and drawing the covers over his head. "Be quiet, will you? You're seriously nuts." Benji's voice was muffled by the covers.

"I'm going," Josh said.

"Don't do it. You'll regret it. I know these things."

"You know how to turn your best friend into a criminal."

"I try to help you and this is what I get. Good night," Benji said, rolling toward the wall.

Josh let himself out and checked both ways down the hall. All was quiet. He tiptoed to Zamboni's room, hesitated, then knocked softly.

Nothing.

Josh looked around and knocked a little louder.

Still nothing.

He thumped the door good this time, rapping loud enough that he was afraid he might wake the entire hall. Vito answered.

"Vito, sorry," Josh said. "I need to talk to Zamboni."

Vito shrugged and let Josh in. The light between the two beds was on. Vito climbed back into bed. Josh shook Zamboni, who groaned and swatted his hand.

"Zamboni," Josh said. "Marcus. I need to talk to you."

"What?" Zamboni said, drawing out the word. "Leave me alone. Are you nuts?"

"You hate my dad. I saw the way you looked at him when we went to Friendly's. And I'm not crazy about your mom, either," Josh said, aware that Vito was looking, but sensing this was his only chance. "But we don't have to hate each other."

"Right," Zamboni said scarcastically.

"I mean it," Josh said. "Truce. We're in the same situation, kind of."

"How are we in the same situation?" Zamboni asked.

"Neither of us wants our families messed up," Josh said, "but they are. Both of us are mad, but we don't have to be mad at each other. That's kind of stupid, really. We can work together. Look at what we do in baseball."

Zamboni wore a look of doubt. "You mean work together, like I don't let your dad know you started a fight that got you kicked out of my room?"

"You started—"

Josh stopped talking. He knew where things would go if he took that path. They'd go back and forth, blaming each other forever.

"It doesn't matter who did what," Josh said, pointing to the red mark on his face. "You punched me. Forget it. We got separated as roommates. Forget it. Let's stop fighting each other. Let's just play baseball and try to win this thing."

Zamboni crossed his arms stubbornly. "It's not easy to just forget."

"I could help you, Zamboni," Josh said. "Like I did with the underhand toss, stuff like that. You're already getting better. And what about your dad? I know you want him to see you play in Williamsport, right?"

Zamboni seemed to consider it, then glanced at Vito. His mouth turned down and he said, "Keep your underhand toss. I'm good enough without your help."

Josh thought about the Skype video and decided to take a chance.

"Right," Josh said, "it's not easy to forget about your mom and my dad and me being wedged into this team at the last minute, but it's also not easy to forget about you smoking in the room all the time, something that would make Vito's dad kick you off this team quick as a hiccup."

"Too bad I don't even smoke," Zamboni said, glancing at Vito, whose head suddenly appeared from beneath his pillow.

Josh grabbed Zamboni's bag off the dresser, dug in, removed Zamboni's cigarettes, and said, "Oh, really? Then how do you explain these?"

Vito sat up straight in his bed, his eyes widening at the cigarettes.

Zamboni narrowed his eyes at Josh, and Josh knew that right then, it was all or nothing.

CHAPTER THIRTY-THREE

JOSH AWOKE EARLY THE next morning and hopped up out of bed, mindful of his promise. He dressed quickly and slipped out of his room. Zamboni was waiting for him in the hallway with his bat bag. Josh nodded to him, and Zamboni followed him down the back stairs and out into the early dawn light, where only the birds were awake.

"You can't use this all the time," Josh said, "but it's a weapon every serious baseball player needs to have."

"I never saw *you* do it," Zamboni said suspiciously.

Josh nodded his head patiently, intent on being nice, telling himself that if he could just get past some rough spots, Zamboni might relax and not sound so nasty.

"I've done it," Josh said, "and I *can* do it, if the coach needs me to."

After showing Zamboni where to stand with his back to the brick wall, Josh knelt down. He picked up a rock and scratched out home plate and a batter's box on the blacktop. Then Josh handed Zamboni his own bat.

"Hold it loose," Josh said, taking it to demonstrate. "Yeah, that's it. Good. Now, you step like this."

Josh showed Zamboni how to step across the plate and drilled him on it again and again.

"When am I gonna bunt it?" Zamboni asked.

"Basics," Josh said, thinking of his father's words.

"Footwork is the key," Josh said. "You gotta have good footwork, or the rest can't follow. You want to be able to lay it down on the third-base line. Come on, give me ten more. Keep the bat loose in your hands. You want it to absorb the force of the ball—that's what dribbles it."

Zamboni did ten more steps and then Josh took a ratty ball he didn't care about from the bottom of his bat bag, pulled on his mitt, and walked out into the parking lot.

"Okay," Josh said. "I'm gonna pitch it. As soon as I get into the back of my windup, you step. Then watch the ball and just move the bat in front of it. You want to connect with the bottom half of the bat. That drives it down. You don't want to pop it up."

Josh threw one in. Zamboni stepped in front of it and the ball hit him square in the gut.

"Ooof," Zamboni said, the air escaping him. "Hey." He raised his bat at Josh, snarling.

"Relax, Zamboni," Josh said. "I'm not trying to hurt

you, just give you a good look. Here, I'll toss some so you can get the idea better."

Josh closed the gap between them and began tossing the ball up. Zamboni missed three times.

"Loosen your shoulders a bit," Josh said.

Zamboni nicked the next one.

"That's it," Josh said. "Now you're on it."

Zamboni's face flickered with a smile that quickly went out.

"Okay," Josh said after Zamboni began to hit it consistently. "Now let me back up."

Josh backed up and began to lob them at the plate. Zamboni missed the first few again but started to connect. Josh repeated the process twice more, finally moving far enough away to mimic a Little League pitcher. Zamboni didn't get it the first day, but they kept at it and four days and four games later, the night before they were to play in the state finals championship game, Josh declared Zamboni ready to bunt.

"All right," Zamboni said, "good.

"One thing I wanted to ask you," Zamboni added as Josh held the door for him to go inside.

"What's up?" Josh asked.

"Call me just Z, will you?" Zamboni said. "I'm not crazy about *Zamboni*. Z is kind of cool, though."

"Well," Josh said, "I'll try."

Zamboni nodded, then asked, "You really think I can bunt tomorrow?"

"I think you can do it, Z," Josh said, "but it'll have to be at the right time. You don't want to go out there every time and try or it won't work, but if we need it, you'll know you've got it in your back pocket."

"How will I know if we need it? Coach Q?"

"Naw," Josh said. "But don't worry. If we need it, I'll tell you."

The next day, in the last inning of the game that would either send them home or on to the regional finals in New Jersey, they needed it.

CHAPTER THIRTY-FOUR

THEY WERE DOWN BY two runs and it was the bottom of the sixth. Zamboni winked at Josh and stepped into the batter's box. Josh gave him a thumbs-up and took a deep breath. A slight breeze lifted Zamboni's hair from his collar. Benji stepped up next to Josh and leaned close.

"Dude, this guy is killing us," Benji said. "What's he batting? One hundred? If he's lucky."

"I think he's gonna get one now," Josh said.

"God knows we need it. Two runs down? We need two of these mopes to get on base and then you get up and do your thing, right?"

"I hope so," Josh said, "but they're not mopes, Benji. Geez, they're our teammates."

"You know what I mean," Benji said. "I'm saying it

with affection. You're a mope half the time and we're like brothers."

Josh smiled and nodded toward Zamboni.

"I told him to bunt."

"Bunt?" Benji said. "To get on base?"

"You don't see a runner to sacrifice over, do you?" Josh said.

"Does he even know how?" Benji asked.

"I taught him."

"What? When?"

"We've been working on it," Josh said.

"You hate that guy."

"I don't hate him," Josh said.

"You don't like him," Benji said.

"I told you. It's part of our agreement. That's how you win, Benji. If you have differences with your teammates, you put them aside. That's how you win championships."

The pitcher wound up and Zamboni stepped across the box.

"There he goes," Benji said.

The ball came fast. Zamboni nicked it perfectly, dribbling it into the no-man's-land between the pitcher, the catcher, and third base. All three defenders ran for the ball and Zamboni took off. The pitcher and the catcher got there at the same time and bumped into each other. The catcher came up with the ball and fired it to first, but not before Zamboni strode over the bag, smacking it with his foot.

"You did it!" Benji said, slapping Josh on the back.

Josh grinned and said, "Actually, *he* did it."

"Now we got a shot," Benji said. "We really got a shot at this. We're at the top of the lineup. One more runner gets on and you can save the day."

"Sure," Josh said, "all I have to do is put it out of the park."

"That's what you do."

Josh studied the sky and said, "Well, Benji, nothing like a little pressure on a sunny day."

CHAPTER THIRTY-FIVE

ZAMBONI TIPPED HIS BATTING helmet to Josh from his spot on second base. Josh adjusted his own batting helmet and returned the gesture, aware that the dreams of the entire team making it to the World Series depended on him. After Zamboni got on base, two batters had struck out before Camren Fries drilled a grounder between the first and second basemen to put himself on first as well as advancing Zamboni to second.

Now Josh was up.

He knew from careful study that the pitcher had all the tricks: sliders, sinkers, curveballs, and even an occasional knuckleball. Josh had started out the game hitting from the left-hand side of the plate, taking away the effectiveness of the right-handed pitcher's curveball. That enabled Josh to get a fastball down the middle in the first inning, a ball he blasted out of the park. Since then, he'd struck out and hit only a double because after Josh's home run, nothing the pitcher threw came down the middle.

Josh stepped into the box on the left-hand side, knowing he needed to somehow drive in three runs if they were to win and advance. The pitcher nodded at his catcher, then threw. Josh swung, even though it was a knuckleball outside. He hit it foul. The next pitch came down the middle but dropped at the last second. Josh swung, barely nicking the top of the ball, foul again.

"Come on, Josh!" Benji screamed from the dugout. "You can do it!"

Josh stepped out of the batter's box and breathed deep. He could hear his father's words in his head.

"Treat every pitch the same. You have to look at an 0–2 count in the bottom of the sixth with two outs the same as the first pitch of the day. That's what the great ones do. Every pitch is the same."

Josh looked up into the stands and saw his dad sitting there with his arm wrapped around Diane's waist. She grinned at Josh and kissed his father's ear. His father gave Josh a serious look and pointed to his own eye.

Josh heard the word "focus" as clearly as if his father had spoken it aloud. He nodded and stepped back into the box, his mind clear of the count and the inning and the outs. Josh knew nothing was coming at him but junk. The pitcher would make him hunt for it, knowing he had three free pitches just to fill the count. But it was late in the game, and Josh also thought that while the pitcher would throw junk, he might be sloppy about it. Lazy. And if he did that, Josh might be able to read the pitch even before it left his hand, read the windup and the way he'd sometimes drop his elbow just a bit on his curveball.

Knowing the pitcher liked his curveball but hadn't been able to throw one to Josh since he'd lined up as a lefty, Josh felt certain that if he switched back to a righty, that was the pitch he'd get. So, Josh circled the plate and stepped into the right-hand box. He thought he saw the shadow of a smile pass briefly across the pitcher's face.

Josh felt the sunshine on his own face and he breathed deep, flexing his fingers, rocking steady in his stance. He didn't try too hard, didn't press—he relaxed and just absorbed the scene in front of him. The pitcher went into his windup. The elbow dropped—the makings of a curve. Josh reset his back foot, stepping toward the plate, opening his stance just enough to catch the meat of a ball breaking to the outside.

The pitch came.

Josh swung.

CHAPTER THIRTY-SIX

THE CRACK OF THE bat and the tremor running through Josh's hands, up his arms, and into his core blasted a smile across his face.

He took off at an easy lope. The crowd stood, cheering. The dugout exploded in wild celebration, sights and sounds Josh could never tire of, never stop aching for. He rounded the bases and let the frenzy swallow him.

When it finally subsided, Josh packed his bag and waded through the crowd of parents toward where his father and Diane and Zamboni stood in the back. Diane was hugging Zamboni and shrieking as if he'd been the one to hit the home run. Josh nodded at his father, and his dad pulled him close with a one-armed squeeze and congratulated him.

"What about Marcus?" Diane asked Josh's dad.

"That was a great bunt," Josh's dad said, shaking Zamboni's hand.

Zamboni's face went red. He nodded toward Josh and reluctantly said, "Josh taught me."

"Josh?" both parents said at the same time.

Josh and Zamboni looked at each other and forced smiles that weren't completely heartfelt, just as they had for the past several days whenever their parents were around. It seemed to be enough, and whenever they did it, the two adults turned their attention to each other. Their adoration made Josh want to throw up, but it beat the alternative of angering his father for not getting along.

"I try to help all the guys," Josh said, not wanting to make a big deal of it. "Stuff I learned from you, Dad. Coach Q is really nice, but I don't know how good of a coach he is."

Josh wanted to change the subject, and on his father's wrist, he saw a brand-new silver watch as big as a plumbing fixture.

"I like that watch, Dad," Josh said.

His father smiled and held it up so that it glinted in the sunlight. "Yeah," he said, "me too. Kind of a present to myself."

"A present?"

"Yes," Diane said, separating herself from Zamboni. "We have a surprise. You two aren't the only big winners. Josh, your father closed a very important deal. As a celebration, Gary and I want to take you two out to a special place. The bankers took us there. It's called Nobu. They have incredible sushi."

Josh shuddered. It was the first time he'd heard Diane call his father Gary. Only Josh's mother called him Gary. Everyone else seemed too afraid to call him anything but Coach or Mr. LeBlanc, and until Josh heard her say his name like that, he still held out hope that Diane wasn't in a position to replace his mom. The sound of her voice and the simpering smile on her face soiled everything. Josh had no desire to go to a place called Nobu and eat raw fish that was likely to make him puke. He wanted to ride the bus home and eat hot pizza with his buddies. Despite the truce he and Zamboni seemed to have come to, Josh couldn't think of many things he'd rather *not* do than ride all the way back to Syracuse in the back of that stupid Audi with him.

"I . . . think Coach Q wants us all to ride with the team." Josh took a quick glance at Zamboni before he continued. "But it sounds great. I'd love to. It's just that my dad always says it's important to be a part of the team, especially since me and Zam—Marcus—scored the winning runs."

Josh put as much pleasant honesty into his expression as he could muster, sensing Diane's careful study, her eyes boring in on him. Josh held her gaze, willing himself not to shudder or blink.

"I think he's right," Zamboni said.

Diane studied her son for a minute, then, finally, a smile crept across her face and she nodded.

"Very nice," she said. "See, Gary, I told you they'd be great friends. Well, we wouldn't want to interfere with your boys' celebration. It's so fantastic to see you two getting along."

Josh didn't know what Zamboni was thinking, but in the privacy of his own mind, he had begun to think of himself as a Trojan horse. Last year in school he'd learned the story of the giant horse the Greek army left as a gift to the Trojans, who brought the horse inside the city gates. That night, the Greek soldiers hidden inside the horse slipped out and opened the city gates from within, allowing the Greek army to enter and destroy the Trojans in their sleep.

That's what Josh wanted to do, get on the inside with Diane, then destroy her when she wasn't ready for it.

CHAPTER THIRTY-SEVEN

IT WAS STRANGE TO Josh, rolling his lawn mower down the sidewalk, working up a grass-stained sweat, and collecting worn-out five- and ten-dollar bills. Everyone in the neighborhood was friendly—except a couple of the dogs bouncing off the inside of their chain-link fences—but no one seemed to be aware of what Josh and his team had done, nor what they were about to do. Oh, the newspaper had allowed Jaden a couple inches of words buried on page eight of the sports section two days ago, but there were no parades, no TV interviews, no general excitement. It was nothing like how it had been after Cooperstown when the Titans competed in and won the Hall of Fame National Championship.

Josh suspected people weren't that interested because they thought it was a fluke or because it didn't really matter that the Lyncourt team was just moving through the Little League qualifying tournaments. All that mattered was whether they made it to the World Series at Williamsport, and then only if they won. That was really it. People didn't put much value on second place or a nice finish, even if no team from Syracuse had ever gone this far before. It was all or nothing.

Either you were the best of the best or you were nothing, and somehow that didn't seem right.

Josh felt his phone vibrate and he read the text from Jaden telling him not to forget that he was her guest reader at the Assisi Center for the little kids after lunch.

"Great," Josh said to himself. He was hot, sweaty, and tired, and now, instead of going home to put his feet up and drink a lemonade, he'd be in the Assisi Center, also hot and also crowded with sweaty little kids crawling all over him as he read them a story.

He didn't bother asking Jaden if he could get out of it. He knew how she felt about the kids at the center—many of them very poor and coming from very difficult situations. Benji only got out of it because he was going with his mom to visit a sick aunt in Rochester, and Jaden said one good deed is as good as another. Besides, her dad had a medical conference he'd taken her to in Toronto, and Josh hadn't seen her since his return from the state finals.

Josh finished his last lawn, got paid, and left the mower behind the garage so he could pick it up later, on his way back from the Assisi Center. Out in the center of the street, heat waffled up from the blacktop. Cars drove past, kicking up grit that made Josh blink and spit. Inside the center's basement, it felt even hotter. The kids were finishing their meal of egg noodles and vegetables, and Jaden offered Josh a plate.

Josh piled the food into his mouth without bothering to sit down. The older kids at the center moved upstairs for some activity of their own. The little kids circled up in a corner onto a rug. Jaden put a copy of *The Sneetches* into Josh's hands and showed him to an upright wooden chair.

"You couldn't have done this?" Josh whispered to her as he eyed the eager cluster of five-, six-, and seven-year-olds.

"The boys need grown-up role models," she said.

"I'm twelve years old."

"But you look older, and I showed them the newspaper articles from when you won the national championship. They think you're famous. Besides, I've got some information for you when we finish."

"About Diane?" Josh asked. "Are you kidding?"

"Hey, I was away."

"Why didn't you text me?"

Jaden shook her head, pressing a finger to her lips and pointing to the kids. "There was nothing you could have done without me but worry, and it's better if no one knows about this. Sometimes people see your texts or you forward them by mistake."

Josh asked, "What you found out about her, is it really that bad?"

Jaden looked into his eyes, showing how serious she was before she said, "It could be a game changer."

CHAPTER THIRTY-EIGHT

JADEN MADE HIM NOT only read but also play Duck, Duck, Goose with the kids before she had a break and could talk with him outside under the shade tree by the swings.

"Are you enjoying this?" Josh said, sitting down on a weathered bench, the wood warm to the touch, even in the shade. "Because I hate this kind of suspense, you know."

"I'm sorry," she answered. "I'm just not going to text this stuff around. It has to stay between us because it's . . . I don't know, weird."

"What is it?"

"All right," she said, sitting next to him. "I think Diane and Zamboni's father are divorced in name only."

"What?" Josh squinted at her. "That makes no sense."

"I'll show you the credit reports I got," she said. "I'm keeping a file at home. They were, like, the poster children for credit card companies. They each had over a dozen, maxed out, totally."

"How do you get this stuff?" Josh asked.

"I'm a reporter." Jaden sounded almost insulted. "With twenty-five bucks and a credit card, you'd be surprised what you can get on the internet. So, they had this business, some kind of natural gas leasing company or something. I don't know. They took a lot of people's money, though, and about a year and a half ago, the whole thing cratered on them."

"But what's that got to do with them not really being divorced?" Josh asked, because that, after all, was what mattered to him most. If Diane was still attached to Zamboni's father, then Josh's dad would be back home before dinner. Josh felt certain of it.

"They moved all the credit cards and the bad business into his name," Jaden said, "then they got divorced, then *he* went bankrupt. I'm not an expert at this stuff. People in the news business call it the money trail—so really, this is great experience for me. Best I can figure, they hid some money and put some things in her name and are just pretending to be divorced so they can get out of paying the people they owe money to."

"But," Josh said, "she's with my dad. They went down to New York City together."

Jaden shrugged. "I don't know about that, but you

know how thorough I am when I do this stuff. Well, I got all kinds of things on the dad in my file, including some old newspaper photos from when he played for the Syracuse Crunch hockey team. His name is Richard Cross, but they called him 'Right.'"

"Right?"

"As in 'right cross,' like a punch. He was a real goon, more penalty minutes and ejections in a single season than any other player in Crunch history."

"Nice," Josh said with sarcasm.

"He's got long blond hair and someone flattened his nose," Jaden said. "So, I'm scoping *her* out at her office. She's got a place on the ground floor in that Nettleton Commons building, the old brick factory they fixed up. About two blocks from my dad's hospital. I was just getting a feel for her, you know, see what she's really up to, and who shows up?"

"Right?"

"Right," Jaden said, "Right Cross, and not just to check on his ex-wife's business prospects. He went in early and stayed late. Lots of people going in and out of that place, too. Mostly men in business suits, but kind of shady looking, like needing a shave or a haircut. I don't know what that means, but it jumped out at me. That was in the morning, then I came to work. When I finished here, I figured I'd just go back by there to see where things were at. I did, and it wasn't long before the two of them came out. Together. With their arms around each other. And then he kissed her like it was some romantic scene in a movie. Your dad can't like that if he's taking her to New York."

"No," Josh said. "He sure can't."

"So," Jaden said, "this is what I'm thinking: These two got into some bad business. They spend money like fiends, money that isn't theirs."

"Buying Audi convertibles," Josh said.

"Yeah, stuff like that," Jaden said, "and when they got in too deep, she takes everything that was worth anything, and he takes all the debts. Everyone lost money but them, and now they're at it again."

Josh snapped his fingers. "They're after my dad."

"Your dad?"

"His Nike contract." Josh felt both excited and sick at the same time. "That's why they went to New York. He said something about getting a bank to give him money in advance for his Nike contract, like four hundred thousand up front, instead of a hundred thousand a year for five years."

"Pledging the money from his contract for a loan?" Jaden said.

"You know what that is?" Josh asked.

"Sure," she said. "I've read about it. It's what you do when you have a big business investment you want to make. It's risky, though. If the investment doesn't work out, you end up working for nothing because the bank takes all the money from the contract."

"What were all those people going into her office for?" Josh asked.

"I don't know," Jaden said. "She *is* a real estate broker. She's closed on some houses, but it's not that. I'm sure. If I had to guess, I'd say Right Cross and Diane went back to what their old company did before it went under."

"What is it? Natural gas?"

"Gas leases," Jaden said. "Hottest thing in New York and the other states to the south. Pipelines going up all over the place. People say there's enough gas underground in New York, Pennsylvania, and West Virginia to put the oil countries like Saudi Arabia out of business for good. What they do is buy leases from people who own the land. They give them money for the right to drill, in case they find gas there. Sometimes you hit a pocket, sometimes you don't. If you do, it's big money. If you don't, you've got nothing. Because it's in the news all the time, lots of people want to invest in it. To me, it sounds like a lottery ticket. Some people are going to make a lot of money, but most are going to wish they'd put it in the bank instead."

"So they're going to try to get my dad to put all his money into this thing." Josh clenched his fists. "Everything he's going to make for the next five years?"

"The question is," Jaden said, "what can we do about it?"

"I can't just say to my dad that he should dump her

because this is what I think she's up to," Josh said. "I know that won't work. Sometimes he giggles when he's with her. He's brain-dead, I'm telling you."

"Then we'll just have to prove it to him."

"Yeah," Josh said. "But how?"

CHAPTER THIRTY-NINE

JADEN REMOVED THE CELL phone from her pocket and said, "Remember how we got the crooked umpire in Cooperstown taking a payoff? We just do *that*." She paused. "What's wrong?"

"I'm not sure," Josh said, "but Benji says taping people like that without them knowing is illegal."

Josh explained how they used Benji's Skype to catch Zamboni on tape smoking in his room.

"Yeah, that's totally illegal," Jaden said. "Every reporter knows that. You can record their voice without them knowing, but you can't take pictures."

"So, how can we take pictures of Diane and Right Cross?" Josh asked.

"Well," she said, "when someone's walking down the street, you can film them. It's when they're someplace where you expect to have privacy, like the bathroom or a hotel room. Those are places you can't record people. These two walked right out onto the sidewalk and started smooching. We get that and it'll blow your dad's mind."

"That's what we've got to get then," Josh said.

"You help me finish out the day here with the kids, and I'll take you to her office. Who knows if they'll both be there, though."

"Well," Josh said, "we have to try."

Josh went back inside with Jaden. They played Charades, and then when there was some extra time at the end, the kids all wanted Josh to read some more, so he did. When the center shut down at four, Jaden and Josh hurried down State Street to the old factory where Diane kept her office. Her white Audi was in the parking lot separated from the street by a black iron fence.

"We're in luck." Jaden nodded toward a black Chevy pickup truck jacked up onto oversized wheels. "That's Right's truck."

"Where you going?" Josh asked.

"Inside." Jaden pointed at the big brick building.

"She'll see me," Josh said.

"She's on the first floor," Jaden said. "We can watch from the balcony above. It's all open. Haven't you ever been in there?"

"No," Josh said. "What if she sees me going in?"

"There are other places in there," Jaden said. "A

clothing store and a bunch of offices. You just say you're with me and I'm shopping. As soon as we're inside, we'll go straight upstairs. The places up there are all empty. No one will see us, but we can see everything from there. Plus, it'll get us close enough to record the mushy stuff."

Thick green vines crept three stories up the side of the old factory. Josh could tell the entrance had been recently added because the bricks were smooth and bright, very different from those in the older part of the building. He was glad for the cool air-conditioned air but nervous that Diane might see him. No excuse Jaden could whip up would make Josh comfortable if he came face-to-face with her in the building where she worked.

"That's it." Jaden angled her head toward a glass storefront in the corner where an empty desk and some plants guarded two separate doorways within. Painted across the glass was CROSS LAND COMPANY.

"That could be homes or that gas lease stuff you talked about," Josh said.

"Exactly."

Arched steel beams rested atop brick columns. Fat globe lights lined the walls, but enough sunlight spilled in through the big windows that they were unneces-sary. The place was quiet except for the secret hiss of the air-conditioning. A few people moved inside the other glass-fronted offices, but the common area was empty. The clack of their feet on the stairs made Josh look around nervously. On the second floor, they found a quiet spot along the gallery and sat down on the wooden floor where they could see the entrance to Diane's office through the bronze railing.

The place was as quiet and cavernous as a library. The few people who did come and go moved quickly and quietly. Josh and Jaden had their backs to a long hallway leading to the fire stairs. They didn't hear anything from that direction until someone cleared his throat and in a growl said, "What are you kids doing here?"

CHAPTER FORTY

JOSH'S MOUTH DROPPED OPEN.

Jaden gasped but then recovered, pushed a finger to her lips, and in a whisper said, "We're keeping an eye on his dad's girlfriend."

The man, whose white hair and mustache made the pink in his weepy eyes seem almost red, gave them a puzzled look.

"Girlfriend?" he asked.

"Shhh. His parents are divorcing and that Cross woman is seeing Josh's dad," Jaden said, nodding toward Josh and explaining away as if she'd been asked the answer to a problem written out on the board in school. "We think she's still with the ex-husband and if we can prove it, Josh's dad might go back with his mom. We're not doing anything wrong—*she* is."

"No one's supposed to be up here," the custodian said, slipping two thumbs into the shoulder straps of his denim overalls.

Jaden looked around. "It's a public place, right? I mean, anyone can come in here to that, like, dress shop, right?"

"Well," the custodian muttered with a nod that shook the loose skin beneath his chin, "I guess I'd have to say it is."

"Yeah, it is," Jaden said, "and we're not hurting anything, right? I mean, if she's really running around like that, there's no sense in letting her break up Josh's family, don't you think? Are you married?"

"Thirty-seven years," the custodian said with pride. "Three kids and two grandkids."

"See?"

"Well." The man scratched the loose skin in his neck. "You just don't get into any trouble then."

"No," Jaden said, shaking her head with a serious face, "we won't."

"And if you need to use the restroom, you use the ones on the first floor. I just cleaned the ones up here."

"Of course," Jaden said.

The man glanced curiously at Josh before disappearing back down the long hall, muttering to himself.

"Are you crazy?" Josh asked in a whisper when the man had disappeared.

"Why am I crazy?" Jaden looked confused.

"You just told that guy why we're here," Josh said. "Who does that?"

"It's always better if you can tell the truth," Jaden said. "People can sense the conviction that you say something with. That's why so many times people know when someone is lying to them. So I told the truth."

"What if he tells her?" Josh asked, nodding down toward Diane's office.

"Him?" she asked, referring to the custodian. "He's married thirty-seven years; you don't think he's on our side?"

"But you didn't know that until you asked him," Josh said impatiently.

Jaden shrugged. "I had a feeling. Call it a woman's intuition."

Josh thought about that in the silence of the building. It wasn't until the inner doors of Diane's office sprang open and four people burst out into the common area that the place exploded with noise. Diane laughed, the sound that somehow had made Josh's father grin. To Josh, it sounded like a crow dropping onto some roadkill from the sky. Her ex-husband spoke in a loud, boastful voice about how smart they all were and how rich they'd soon become. The other two were both men, looking—as Jaden had said—somewhat suspicious and in need of grooming. Their faces were flushed with excitement, though, as they nodded and shook hands with the Crosses before leaving the building.

Diane and her ex-husband watched them go, then turned to each other, shaking hands on some deal of their own before Right bent over and kissed her. Josh looked over at Jaden, who eagerly held her phone out through a space in the railing, directing its lens at the couple. Josh looked back down, but the Crosses had already separated. The ex-husband crossed the lobby and left while Diane went back inside her office.

"Did you get it?" Josh whispered.

"I think so." Jaden fumbled with her phone and held the screen up for Josh to look at, too. "Let's see."

CHAPTER FORTY-ONE

JOSH STUDIED THE TINY screen, watching for the second time as the Crosses emerged from the office with their clients or victims or whoever they were.

"You can see it's them, right?" Jaden asked.

"I think so," Josh said. "And you can hear that stupid laugh that he loves so much. Yeah, he'll know it's her."

They watched the departure of the two men and then the kiss.

"The other day," Jaden said, "they were really going at it, but a kiss is a kiss, right? No way is your dad going to go for this. It proves they're still together."

"I don't think so either," Josh said, shaking his head as he imagined one of his father's angry faces.

"So, we got it." Jaden snapped her phone shut.

"Can I take it?" Josh asked. His own phone was a

basic model without a camera or video capabilities. "I'll give you mine to use."

"Sure," Jaden said, handing it over and taking Josh's phone in return. "When are you going to show it to him?"

"He's supposed to pick me up for dinner, then go to the batting cage. When he sees this, I bet he's back home before I leave for the regionals tomorrow morning."

Jaden looked at him, her face suddenly blank.

"What?" Josh asked.

"I don't know," she said. "I'm having second thoughts. Maybe we should get more proof. Something like I saw the other day. Maybe a couple of times. People are funny about this stuff. Sometimes they believe what they want to believe instead of what they see. You've heard of the saying 'Don't shoot the messenger,' right?"

"Yeah, but what's that got to do with this?" Josh asked.

"I just don't want this to backfire on you," Jaden said. "Maybe it's just because what I saw the other day was so much more mushy than what they just did. I mean, they had their hands all over each other."

"Don't worry." Josh held up the phone. "This is enough. Trust me. Let's get out of here."

Jaden followed him down the stairs. He checked Diane's office. The inner door was closed, so he knew she was in the back. They scooted across the lobby and outside into the heat. They walked up the hill together, passing the hospital, then Jaden kept going toward her own house while Josh took a left after thanking her for saving his life.

"Okay," Jaden said. "I hope it works."

"Don't worry." He grinned. "It's guaranteed."

Josh retrieved his lawn mower and pushed it back to the garage behind his house. The smell of cut grass drifting up from the lawn mower's blade made him think of baseball and the contest just around the corner that was so big it made him shiver. He ached to get there, to a place where kissing grown-ups and unpaid bills were replaced by fastballs, double plays, and home runs.

When he went inside, his mom was at the kitchen table sorting through a pile of papers with a big blue binder full of checks in the middle of it all. She chewed on the end of a pen and studied some numbers with a frown.

"Mom?" Josh said, startling her.

"Hi, honey," she said. "I didn't hear you come in. These bills."

"Everything okay?" he asked.

"Oh, we'll make it," she said, forcing a smile. "I thought things would finally get easier when your father got that Nike contract is all."

Josh wondered if his mom somehow knew about Diane's whole scheme and that the contract might be at risk, and he asked, "That's not going away, right?"

"No," she said, "I can't see how that could happen. It's a five-year deal, but having that money for one family isn't the same as two."

"Two?"

"Us," she said, "and your father."

"He doesn't have another family," Josh said, panicked at the thought of his father actually marrying Diane and being Zamboni's dad, too.

"Not a whole family," his mom said, "yet. But we still need money for two of almost everything. Two homes. Two cars. Two grocery bills, two light bills, cable TV, insurance, all that. Things will be tight again. That's why I have to find a job. I feel bad not being able to go and support you, Josh. You know I don't usually miss your games, but things aren't usual anymore. I've *got* to find work."

It looked like his mom was close to tears. Josh stuck a hand in his pocket and caressed Jaden's cell phone.

"Mom," he said. "I think I can fix everything."

"What?" she said, her face rumpling like the blanket on an unmade bed. "What are you talking about, Josh?"

Josh took the cell phone out of his pocket and held it up with his heart racing in his chest like a cluster of brightly colored NASCAR racers taking a turn at a hundred and fifty miles an hour. He opened the phone, punched up the video, and handed it to her so that all she had to do was hit the play button.

"This," Josh said proudly. "I've got a video of that Diane with her ex-husband. If Dad thinks she's his, well, this proves she's not. They're divorced, but they're still together. When he sees *this*, he'll be back here before you know it. I know Dad. I'm sure he will."

Josh looked eagerly at the expression on his mom's face, which changed from puzzled to deeply sad.

"Why are you looking at me like that?" Josh asked.

His mom slowly closed the phone and handed it back to him. "I'm sorry, Josh. I know how bad you'd like everything to go back to the way it was, but that's just not possible."

"Mom," Josh said, his vision blurring with tears of his own as he clutched the phone, "I'm telling you, he'll come back."

"Even if he wanted to," she said, shaking her head, "he can't."

Josh's throat tightened so that he had trouble getting the words out. Finally they came.

"But why?"

CHAPTER FORTY-TWO

"I CAN'T JUST TAKE him back, Josh," his mother said. "Even if your plan worked."

"I don't understand."

"I know you don't." His mom threw her hands up in the air. "It's an adult thing, but when one person breaks up a marriage for someone else, the person left behind can't just take them back. Once a marriage is broken, there's no more trust. The person who got betrayed has almost nothing left emotionally. It's extremely painful, Josh. The one thing I have is my pride, and I can't just give that away, too."

"Pride?" Josh said, repeating it as if to himself.

"Your father can't just come and go, Josh. No one can live that way," she said. "We have real problems between us—things about him and me—that need to be fixed before it could ever work. Trust me, the only thing worse than what you and Laurel and I are feeling right now would be if we had to go through it all again. We'll get through this. We'll heal, but we can't keep opening the wounds. You can't live your life in a constant state of bleeding."

"You make it sound like a war or something," Josh said.

"It's worse than war," his mom said, gripping the pen and pointing it at him so that the soft blue veins stood out in her hands. "At least in war, you know the enemy going in. This is when the person you love and trust with your life walks away from you. It's much worse. I know it might be hard for you to understand."

"You're right," Josh said, waving the phone in the air. "It *is* hard for me to understand. I'm just a kid who plays baseball. I only know that when you want to win, you have to do things that aren't always easy. Well, I want us to be together again. I want you to do something that might not be easy for you, but we all win in the end if you do."

"This has nothing to do with baseball, Josh," she said sharply, pointing the pen at her heart as if to stab it. "This is life."

"It's supposed to be the same, isn't it?" Josh said. "That's what every coach I've ever had has said, even Dad."

"Do you think baseball is the same as life?"

"No," Josh said, "baseball is way better. You know what you have to do and you either do it and you win, or you don't and you lose. You know who's for you because you all wear the same colors. Nobody changes teams during a baseball game."

"Well," she said, "in life, sometimes people change teams."

"Then you know what?" Josh asked.

"What?"

"Life stinks." Josh turned and sprinted out the kitchen door, slamming it shut before running down the driveway. When he reached the sidewalk, he went left and kept going with the phone clutched tight in his hand, his vision blurry, running toward a place he didn't know.

CHAPTER FORTY-THREE

JOSH WANDERED THROUGH THE streets in the late afternoon heat, his head down. He found a stick and dragged it along the brick walls of the buildings on State Street, circling the people who lay in the shaded entryways of abandoned storefronts. Cars and trucks swept past, whipping up hot, grit-filled air in their paths. After a time Josh found himself under the highway. The traffic roared overhead, and the cavern of steel and concrete below moaned and groaned as if in pain.

Finally Josh sent a text to his own phone so Jaden would know he was on his way, then hurried along, winding through the city until he arrived at her house.

"Here," he said, handing her the phone, "you might as well take it back."

"Did you show him? What happened?" she asked, letting him in.

"It's no use," Josh said, flopping down on her couch, the cool air from a window air conditioner blowing through his hair.

"Why not?" Jaden asked, sitting down beside him.

Josh told her what happened with his mom.

Jaden stared at the phone in her hand and shook her head slowly as she said, "I never even thought of that, your mom *not* wanting him back."

"It's not that she doesn't want him," Josh said. "Just not until they work things out, their problems, whatever those are."

Jaden returned the phone to him and said, "But maybe this can get it started. I mean, it's not an instant solution, but you keep saying you can't stand Diane, and if he's with her, there isn't even a chance they'll work things out, right?"

"I guess not." Josh slipped the phone into his pocket.

"Of course not," she said.

"I don't know." Josh shook his head.

"You've got nothing to lose," Jaden said. "Why wouldn't you?"

"I don't know," Josh said again. "He's not going to be happy to see this. I've got to get ready for these regional finals, and I need time in the batting cage. He's supposed to take me to dinner, then to the Titans' batting practice he's got lined up tonight. I don't want him to freak out on me and cancel everything."

"But it happened, right?" Jaden said. "You're not making up a story or spreading some rumor. This is cold, hard evidence. Nothing is your fault."

Josh thought for a minute, then looked at the clock on her father's desk.

"Will you do it with me?" he asked.

"Me? How?"

"I can call him right now to come over here," Josh said.

"I don't think I should be the one to tell him," Jaden said.

"You don't have to say anything. Just be here with me."

"Sure," she said. "I will."

Josh dialed his father, who said it wasn't a problem at all for him to come a little early and to pick him up at Jaden's.

"I've got something to show you," Josh said.

"That's funny," his father said, "because I've got something to show you, too."

Josh hung up, and he and Jaden looked at each other.

"You want to listen to some CDs?" she asked.

"Sure."

Josh had no idea what they listened to because he was really listening for the doorbell. When it rang, he jumped up and swung open the door. His father stepped in, filling the entryway and ducking his head so as not to collide with the light that hung from a brass chain. Josh turned and went back into the living room, sitting down on the couch and grabbing Jaden's cell phone up off the coffee table.

"So," his father said in that deep rumble as he passed through the doorway and stood with his arms folded across his massive chest, "what is it you want me to see?"

CHAPTER FORTY-FOUR

"DAD," JOSH SAID, HOLDING up the phone. "I don't want you to shoot the messenger."

"Why would I?" his dad asked. "What are you two up to?"

Jaden sat with her hands pinned under her legs and her mouth clamped shut. She looked from Josh to his dad and back with wide eyes.

"Do you want to sit down, Dad?" Josh asked, his voice now trembling. He felt like the Athenians must have felt inside their Trojan horse, inside the city walls, ready and waiting to spring out and grab the victory they deserved.

"Not really," his father said. "What have you got there?"

"There's a clothing store in Nettleton Commons,"

Josh said, nodding at Jaden. "I went there with Jaden after helping out at the Assisi Center."

"They have great tops," Jaden said, "lots of silk. Stuff from New York City."

"And so," Josh said, looking at the phone in his hands. "We were there. And we were in the gallery upstairs and, I don't know, we were sitting and talking, and all of a sudden Diane comes out of what I guess is her office."

"Right," his dad said, "that's where she works. So what?"

"Well, Dad," Josh said, standing up and crossing the small room so he could hand over the phone. "I had Jaden's phone and I saw Diane with this guy who I guess is her ex-husband and . . ."

Josh started to choke on his words. He didn't know which strangled him more, fear or embarrassment. Either way, he was out of the horse now. No more surprise attacks. The fight was on.

"And, what?" his dad asked.

"Just play it. You'll see. Just hit the play button."

His father set his jaw, scowling and frowning and immovable as he hit the play button. Josh could hear the audio of Diane's cackle and the boastful sound of Right Cross, her ex-husband. Josh snuck a peek at his father's face when it got to the part where he knew they kissed, then he looked down.

His father snapped the phone shut with a cold and

final pop. Josh looked up. His father held out the phone to him and took a deep breath, filling his lungs with a sound that reminded Josh of when they filled the propane tanks for their grill. Josh took the phone and waited.

CHAPTER FORTY-FIVE

"I'M CERTAINLY NOT GOING to shoot the messenger," his father finally said.

Josh looked up. None of the anger had lost its hold on his father's concrete face. The thick black brows still met at angles on the bridge of his nose like two caterpillars diving for the same spot.

"Good," Josh said quietly. "I mean, I'm sorry about all this, but I thought you'd want to know."

"You're right," his father said. "I'd rather know than not."

"So, what will you do?" Josh asked.

"End it."

Those two words seemed to hang in the air.

"End it?" Joy bloomed inside of him. "For real?"

"Sometimes you think you know someone," his father

said, "but when you find out you can't trust them, it's never the same."

Josh winced at the similarity of what his father said to what his mother had told him only an hour ago.

"What?" his father demanded.

Josh hesitated, then looked down and said, "Mom said the same thing about you."

Josh's dad glanced at Jaden and bit into his lower lip. "Listen, Josh. I know you don't understand any of this, but sometimes things happen with two people. It's hard to explain. You'll understand when you're older."

His father looked past him, staring out the window for a minute as if in deep thought before he said, "Anyway, let's go hit some balls. Whatever happens with all this, the Titans have a tournament in Cleveland this weekend and then Philadelphia the next week. Without you and Benji, we need all the practice we can get. And you've got the regional finals. If you win, you'll go to the World Series. Think about *that*, not all this other stuff. That's something you'll remember for the rest of your life."

"I don't care about the World Series, Dad," Josh said. "It's one tournament."

"Don't say that, Son," his father said. "You think that now, but believe me, the day will come when all this stuff with me and your mother will fade, but playing in the World Series will be right there in the front of your mind as long as you live."

"But I'd give it up in a second to have you and Mom back together," Josh said.

His father's concrete expression seemed like it might crumble, and Josh thought he saw the glint of moisture in his eyes, but all his father said was "Let's go."

His father turned toward the door, then looked back and said, "Jaden, why don't you come have dinner with us at Aunt Josie's? I talked to Pops—he's got some homemade noodles and braciole."

Jaden shrugged and said, "Okay, sure. Thanks, Mr. LeBlanc. My dad has rounds until nine, so I was on my own."

"Now you're with us," Josh's dad said.

Outside in Jaden's driveway sat a brand-new red Camaro with tan leather seats.

"Wow," Josh said, despite remembering his mother's words about them not having enough money, "nice."

"I thought you'd like it," his father said, obviously proud.

They had dinner and then went straight to the batting cages, where Jaden helped Josh's dad keep stats on the team's batting as he went through the cages coaching them, one by one. Josh felt his rhythm and his dad only stayed in his cage for half a dozen balls before he nodded at Josh and said, "Just keep doing what you're doing, Josh."

Jaden grinned and followed Josh's dad to the next cage.

Josh turned his attention back to the machine, switching off from left to right and blasting nearly everything that came at him. With every pitch, he felt a bit of steam from his anger and anxiety released into the summer twilight, drifting up to mix with the bugs that swarmed the halogen lights high above the cages. When he finally walked out of the cage, tugging his hand free from the batting glove, he felt tired and almost at peace.

It seemed to him that once his father ditched Diane Cross, everything would work out. It might take his mom some time to get over the hurt, but, like Jaden said, sooner or later she had to come around. That's how it seemed to Josh as he and Jaden and his dad rode through the streets with the windows down, eating ice-cream cones and bobbing their heads to the sound of the radio. When they dropped Jaden off, she was so giddy she wished Josh good luck and kissed his cheek before skipping up the steps and into her house.

Josh blushed and stayed silent as his father rumbled through the streets. When they pulled up in front of their house, Josh asked, "You want to come in?"

CHAPTER FORTY-SIX

HIS FATHER TURNED THE radio off and chuckled, messing up Josh's hair.

"You never stop, right?" he said. "I like your persistence, buddy, but you have to understand that this isn't something you can just badger back into place. It's a mess. I don't know what's going to happen, but I know whatever it is, it's not your fault."

Josh hung his head.

"Do you think that?" his dad asked. "That it's your fault?"

Josh cleared his throat and softly said, "I just can't help thinking how things would be if we didn't win in Cooperstown. Then you wouldn't have even been looking for a new house. That's how you met Diane. It never would have happened."

His father took a deep breath and let it out slow. "You can't go through life like that, Son. You do your best. You try. But you have to know when things are beyond your control."

Josh looked up at the house, knowing from the glow in the front window that the TV was on, probably Gran, and the bathroom light upstairs meant his mom was giving Laurel a bath.

"I still don't want you to be with someone who's going to do what she's doing," Josh said. "And if that ends, you can't blame me for thinking about you guys getting back together."

"No," his father said, "I guess I can't blame you. But I've got to find out what's really going on."

"Isn't it obvious?" Josh asked.

"Not always, Josh," his father said.

"You're kidding," Josh said.

"Look," his dad said, taking hold of Josh's shoulder, "first things first. Let me deal with Diane. Even if it turns out things are as bad as they seem, I need to end it the right way. Then let me go hopefully try to win this tournament in Ohio. Without you it won't be easy. Then, when I get back, I can try to talk with your mom. I don't want you to get your hopes up, though."

"So if it's true," Josh said, "you're gonna dump that Diane like a bad habit, right?"

His father looked out at the street ahead. Bugs streaked through the headlight beams.

"I guess, something like that," his father said. "It's

not going to happen tonight, though. She's at some Realtors conference in Pittsburgh. I'll talk to her when I get back from the tournament."

"If we do win this thing," Josh said, feeling better and better about everything, "you won't even be able to see the World Series, will you? You've got the Philadelphia tournament coming up."

"Hey," his dad said, squeezing Josh's shoulder so hard it almost hurt. "You make it to the World Series, I'll figure something out. It's not too far from there to Williamsport, and that's not something I want to miss. I'm telling you, don't be distracted by all this. Think about playing the best of the best in the entire *world*. We talk about scouts and all the people who saw you at Cooperstown and that was great. No doubt you're on people's radar screens, but this will lock you into those people's minds. You do *this* and I promise you, you'll have a Division One scholarship with your name on it. After that, straight to the pros."

Josh felt an electric current pass through him and it was as if he were floating off the seat.

"You good?" his dad said, meaning did Josh understand what was at stake.

"Yeah," Josh said, "I just wish you were coaching us instead of Coach Q."

His father nodded, then said, "You coach them. You coached Marcus to bunt. You know the game as well as anyone."

"I . . . " Josh said. "I kind of am already."

Josh told him about some of the things he'd done.

"See?" his dad said. "So, step it up. Keep coaching them. Don't be shy about it."

"But I don't think Coach Q would like it," Josh said. "He likes calling it his team."

"It can be his team," Josh's dad said. "I didn't say it couldn't. You didn't either. But you can get those guys ready. Just be discreet."

"Like, keep it secret?" Josh asked.

"It's not that you have to keep it a secret," his dad said. "Just be, I don't know, *quiet* about it."

"Okay," Josh said, grinning. "I like it. Coaching. Just like you."

"Well, not just like me," his dad said.

"Why not?"

"If a player is on my team, he knows I'm the coach. You're a player, so you have to be careful that they *want* your help. Does that make sense?"

"Sure," Josh said.

"Good," his dad said, "because if you get it wrong, you'll wish you never tried."

CHAPTER FORTY-SEVEN

IN THE FIRST GAME of the regional finals in New Jersey, Josh blasted a grand slam in the top of the sixth inning that gave his team a two-run lead. That's how the side ended, and the Lyncourt All-Stars took the field in the bottom of the inning chattering like parakeets and confident they could defeat the team from Orchard Park. Niko Fedchenko took the mound. He was as hot as a chili pepper.

As they threw the ball around the infield to warm up, Josh sensed a joyful carelessness in his teammates that sat in his stomach like a spider. His prior experience—first with a U14 team, then with the National Champion Titans—had taught him never to relax until the final out of the game. His teammates, however, seemed to feel like the bottom of the sixth was nothing more than an opportunity to show the parents and fans in the stands how easy it was for them to beat Orchard Park.

"Guys!" Josh shouted as the first batter stepped up to the plate. "Come on, let's finish this out. Everybody on their toes!"

"Josh!" Benji shouted from right field. "Like this?"

Benji made a show of rising up on his tippy toes before he cut a loud fart. The entire team broke out into a fit of laughter, including Niko on the mound. Josh shook his head and got into his spot on the edge of the infield halfway between second and third.

Niko lobbed one in and the first batter smacked it deep into right field. Benji backpedaled like a champion and snagged the pop fly, hooting like a maniac as he fired the ball back into the infield.

One out. Still, Josh felt like his uniform was two sizes two tight and he wiped a patch of sweat from his forehead. He knew the casual attitude of his teammates was a dangerous thing. Niko blew a kiss to someone in the crowd before he threw his first pitch to the next batter. The Orchard Park second baseman blasted the pitch into the hole between first and second and bounced on his own toes as he stood safely on first.

"Come on, guys!" Josh shouted. "Let's lock this thing down."

Niko looked at Josh, this time more serious. The pitcher seemed to focus and threw two straight strikes before two balls and finally a fastball that left the batter swinging and missing. Two outs.

Niko grinned at Josh and offered a thumbs-up. Coach Q howled from the dugout. "Get 'em, Niko! You're the man!"

Niko took the praise to heart and fooled around with the next batter enough that a missed pitch got by Vito and the runner on first stole second.

"Enjoy the exercise!" Benji shouted to the runner on second. "'Cause you ain't gettin' home."

"Benji!" Josh shouted. "You see that batter? That's the tying run. Focus on him and let's get this win."

"We got the win, buddy!" Benji shouted. "We got it locked down tighter than a beetle's butt crack."

The laughter from all sides only made Josh clench his teeth and shake his head. The batter stepped into the box and Josh recognized the other team's big first baseman, who'd already hit a triple in the second inning. Josh glanced at the runner on second and stepped back a bit onto the grass. Niko wiped a tear of laughter from his eye and wound up for the pitch.

The crack of the bat startled even Josh. The ball disappeared into the sky, nearly straight up, but hit so hard that it would surely come down outside the infield. The runner on second took off. Josh reacted instinctively, moving into position to cover second as the second baseman ran for the pop fly. As the second baseman moved back, Benji shot forward, as did the center fielder.

All three players shouted at the tops of their lungs,

"I got it! I got it! I got it!"

As the ball was falling to the earth, Josh was aware of the batter cruising toward him after rounding first and the other runner rounding third on his way home. If Benji caught it, the game would be over. If not, it'd be bad news.

As the batter flashed past second, Josh surged toward the outfield without thinking. Benji's glove went up, but so did the second baseman's as well as the center fielder's. At the same instant Zamboni sprinted into the scene all the way from left field. When all four players collided, the ball bounced off the heap and dribbled to the ground, uncaught, and with the batter headed for home.

CHAPTER FORTY-EIGHT

JOSH GOT THERE BEFORE any of his four teammates could recover. He snatched the ball from the grass, cranked his hips around, and fired a rocket for home plate. The batter whose run would have tied the game slid, low and hard, with picture-perfect form. The ball snapped home into Vito's catcher's mitt. A cloud of dust exploded from beneath the runner's feet and the umpire dipped his head toward the plate, pausing to be certain of what he'd seen.

Josh held his breath.

The entire stadium went quiet. Josh heard the voice of a little kid somewhere in the stands asking his parent what happened.

"You're out!" shouted the umpire.

Josh's team exploded with cheers, and Coach Q

danced out onto the field to hug his son. Josh hooted and jumped into the air, slapping high-fives with Niko. From the corner of his eye he caught the flash of someone from the crowd leaping over the fence. Josh turned and watched as Diane Cross dashed out onto the grass, sprinting on high heels toward the pile of players behind second base who were still recovering from their crash.

"Marcus! Marcus!" Diane screeched, dropping to her knees and taking Zamboni's face in her hands. "Oh my God! Someone get an ambulance!"

"Mom!" Zamboni said, slapping away her hand and shaking free from her grip. "Cut it out. I'm fine."

"Look at that lump!" she said. "You are *not* fine. Coach Q! An ambulance!"

Benji, the center fielder, and the second baseman all got to their feet, dusting themselves off and looking embarrassed, not only for their own comical collision, but for Zamboni's hysterical mom.

Josh could see the purple knot on Zamboni's forehead from where he stood, and when he saw Benji rubbing the side of his own head, Josh thought he knew what had happened and went over to his friend to ask if he was okay.

"Me?" Benji said. "I'm fine. Made of bricks, you know that."

"Bricks in your brain," Josh said, grinning.

"I was talking about the outside," Benji said, flexing a muscle. "Nice work cleaning up the mess. I told you we had this thing locked up."

"That was too close." Josh glanced at home plate, where Coach Q had let go of Vito. The coach marched out to where they stood next to Zamboni and his mom.

"Aww," Benji said, swatting the air, "we gave the crowd a little drama. That's what champions do. Come on, let's get away from this soap opera."

Josh glanced over at Zamboni and his mom, thankful for Zamboni's sake that she'd finally quieted down. Josh agreed with Benji by motioning his head and moving toward the dugout.

After they had their bags packed and slung from their shoulders, Josh, Benji, and the rest of the players headed for the team bus. Zamboni continued to shoo his mom away, but she buzzed around him like a pesky mosquito until he stepped up onto the bus holding an ice pack onto his forehead while half the team stuffed knuckles in their mouths to keep from giggling at him.

"Can I sit here?" Zamboni asked Josh.

Josh got up so Zamboni could slide into the window seat. Benji sat across the aisle and rolled his eyes at Josh. Josh shrugged, and Zamboni rested his head against the window until his mom began tapping at the glass from the outside and he turned his back to her, shaking his head. Zamboni looked at Josh with red cheeks.

"It's no big deal," Josh said, touching the scar below his eye. "You should have seen my mom when I got this. Right, Benji?"

Benji yawned.

"Anyway," Josh said, "we need to work out who does what on a pop fly."

"Who does what?" Benji asked, narrowing his eyes.

"There are rules for who can call off the other players," Josh said.

"Isn't it just whoever calls it?" Zamboni asked.

"Not really," Josh said. "Because then you get situations like we just had, and that's not good. It's not a big deal, but let's get everyone together before tomorrow's game and get it straight, that's all."

"The whole team?" Benji asked.

"Why not?" Josh asked. "It's something everyone needs to know. We can meet in the parking lot before dinner. I can go over it and we'll be all set."

Benji nodded and so did Zamboni. When they got back to the hotel, the word spread that everyone was going to meet in the parking lot behind the hotel at five forty-five, right before dinner. When Josh arrived, there were already a handful of guys there, and soon the whole team arrived, standing in a cluster around Josh.

"Okay," Josh said, "it's no big deal, but we've all got to be on the same page when there's a pop fly so we don't get a repeat of today."

"How do you know?" someone asked from the back.

Josh felt his face grow warm, but before he could say anything, Benji stepped up.

"Because me and Josh are the playmakers, that's

how he knows," Benji said, jutting out his jaw in the direction the question had come from. "And if anyone's got a problem, let me know right now."

No one said anything, but there was a general murmur of acceptance.

"Guys," Josh said, "I'm just trying to help us win."

The metal door from the back stairwell to the hotel suddenly banged open. Everyone turned to see Vito and his dad emerge. Coach Q scowled.

Vito pointed at Josh and said, "See, Dad? This guy thinks *he's* the coach."

All eyes turned back to Josh.

CHAPTER FORTY-NINE

JOSH'S MOUTH FELL OPEN, but no words came out.

"What are you doing, LeBlanc?" Coach Q asked, stuffing his hands into the pockets of his pants.

Josh looked toward the ground and said, "Just trying to help, Coach."

"With what?" Coach Q asked.

"Just the rules on a pop fly," Josh said, his voice barely a mutter.

"There are no rules," Coach Q said. "Whoever calls it gets it. It's simple."

Josh looked up at Coach Q's round red face and saw from the look in his eyes that he really didn't know.

"Coach," Josh said, "all due respect, but I'm pretty sure there are."

"Oh!" Coach Q said with a burst of laughter. "Really?"

"Well," Josh said, glancing around to see that his

teammates were paying attention. “If it’s in the infield, it’s the shortstop’s call. If he calls it, everyone else has to back off.”

Coach Q let loose another burst of laughter before he said, “Don’t you think you make enough plays, Josh? Now you gotta have the clout to call everyone off on a pop fly? Come on.”

“Not because I’m the shortstop, Coach,” Josh said, his face burning now at the chuckles from his team. “If it goes outside the infield, even an inch, then any outfielder can call off any infielder.”

Doubt flickered on Coach Q’s face, but he kept his smile going and said, “That doesn’t help if it’s between two outfielders like today, so your rules don’t help too much.”

Josh shook his head. “If it’s in the outfield and it’s between two of them, the center fielder can call off either of the other two. That’s the rule.”

Coach Q’s smile faded. Everyone watched as Coach Q’s face changed from white, to purple, then back to red.

After another moment of silence, he said, “That’s the rule they use in the major leagues.”

“Yeah,” Josh said in what was barely a whisper, uncertain of how the whole thing would end.

Finally the coach said, “Not something I was sure you kids were ready for, but . . . Excellent. Good idea to get everyone together. Great. Okay, everyone clear on the rules?”

Coach Q looked around at the silent faces, then clapped his hands and said, "Great. All right. Here we go. Time for dinner."

Everyone followed the coach and his son back into the hotel. Josh leaned close to Benji's ear and said, "Playmakers? Where'd you get that?"

"Hey," Benji whispered back. "That's what we are, dude. I wasn't going to let anyone call what you had to say into question. You and me? We're alpha males. These mutts don't question us. Do I gotta teach you everything?"

"I guess everything but the rules on a pop fly," Josh said, and Benji returned his grin before punching him softly in the shoulder.

After dinner they were already in bed when Josh's phone rang. The sight of his home number filled him with unease.

"Josh?"

"Hi, Mom," he said.

"You didn't call," she said.

"I know you're busy," he said. "We won."

"That's great," she said. "I won, too."

"You won? Won what?"

"I just got off the phone with the owner of Murray's Catering," his mom said, speaking so quickly she was nearly out of breath. "Josh, I got a job!"

She sounded so happy, Josh had to grin.

CHAPTER FIFTY

THE GOOD LUCK JOSH'S mom experienced seemed to spread.

The next day Josh and Benji's team won by two runs. The day after that, they won by three. In all the excitement, everyone seemed to forget about the pop fly rules and Josh's uncomfortable exchange with Coach Q. It seemed like their team was destined to win the regionals and make it to Williamsport.

But on the third day, in the semifinal game of the regional qualifiers, the Lyncourt All-Stars found themselves in a bind. They had a one-run lead, and it was the bottom of the sixth with two outs. The problem was that the bases were loaded. That's when a pop fly went high over second base, and Josh sprang into action.

"I got it!" Josh yelled, calling off the second baseman.

In the back of Josh's mind, he congratulated himself

when the second baseman stepped away because of the talk they'd all had. The ball sailed up so far that it looked like a pinprick in the sky. Josh stood solidly beneath it in the grass just beyond second base, even before it began to drop. When it was halfway to his glove, Josh heard Zamboni running his way at full speed, shouting, "I got it! I got it! I got it!"

Josh bit his lower lip. There was no way he wouldn't make this catch, end the game, and send them into the finals but he remembered his own rules. Josh glanced at Zamboni, and, even though Zamboni's chances of making the play didn't look good, he stepped clear of the ball.

Zamboni, whose eyes were intent on the ball, dove with an outstretched glove. Josh winced, almost certain now that Zamboni couldn't make the catch. They'd lose, and everyone would go home, destroying the only chance they'd ever have of playing in the World Series.

It would all be Josh's fault for being too smart for his own good and coaching his own team with an advanced set of rules they obviously weren't ready for.

CHAPTER FIFTY-ONE

ZAMBONI CLIMBED UP OFF the ground, looking directly at Josh. The egg on his forehead had shrunk to a small rise and the purple had faded to a sickly yellow and black.

"Sorry, Josh," he said.

Josh felt his own face stretch into a gigantic smile.

"Don't say you're sorry, Z," Josh said, clapping his teammate on the shoulder. "We just won!"

Everyone crowded around Zamboni, thumping him on the back as he held the ball for all to see before handing it to Josh.

When they all got to the dugout, Coach Q put an arm around Josh and said, "Good thing we went over those pop fly rules, right?"

"Great thing, Coach," Josh said.

"Great thing," Coach Q said, grinning. "We won the game, and I made a big sale when I got that call in the bottom of the third inning. I just covered your first year of college, Vito. It's definitely time to celebrate!"

"But not too much, right, Coach?" Josh said.

"Hey, Josh, it's not every day you sell a Gullwing convertible." Coach Q winked and said, "But today doesn't mean anything if we don't get the job done tomorrow, right, Josh?"

"Absolutely," Josh said.

Coach Q nodded, then turned to the team and raised his voice. "Guys, enjoy the win. The pizza and sodas are on me, and then it's to bed. Don't forget, as nice as this win was, it's all about tomorrow."

Tomorrow came fast, and in the regional finals the Lyncourt All-Stars had a one-run advantage in the bottom of the last inning. The bad news was that the momentum had turned against them completely, and the hope of hanging on to their lead was fading fast.

This time Josh's teammates remembered the close call they had in the opening game, so no one was goofing around. Even with a one-run lead and two outs, they stood in the field, jittery, palms sweating and almost in a daze. The sound of the cheering crowd swept past them like a swift current. Josh's arms and legs seemed to float on the little swirls of heat kicking up dust devils on the infield grit.

"Come on!" Benji shouted, his voice hoarse from a

week's worth of shouting and laced with desperation because things were so obviously slipping away. "We got this! This is ours!"

Josh glanced at his friend for an instant before his eyes took in the runners in scoring position on second and third and the batter in the box who'd already hit a double and a home run in the game. Callan Fries checked Josh from his spot on the mound. Josh signaled for him to throw only junk, knowing their best bet was to either strike him out swinging at a bad pitch or load up the bases and go after the next batter.

Callan was shaken after giving up three runs already this inning, but he nodded and went into his windup. He delivered a sinker that hit the plate and took a wild bounce. Josh saw the runner on third start to go. The catcher leaped up, whipping off his mask and diving for the ball. Josh moved without thinking, knowing the place for him was backing up the third baseman in case they stopped the runner and got him into a pickle. Even as he ran, Josh realized it was hopeless. The catcher could never reach the ball in time. Sickness hit Josh like a brick.

Then they got lucky.

With nothing between him and home plate but the chalk baseline, the runner tripped and fell and Vito reached for the ball, snatching it from the dirt and starting fast toward home plate, the ball in his glove, both hands stretching to tag the runner. The runner bounced up and realized he wouldn't make it to the plate before Vito.

He turned and sprinted back for third. Vito ran three steps down the baseline and fired for third so the third baseman could tag him out. The throw was high and wild. The third baseman jumped and missed and the runner turned and dashed for home. Josh leaped for the ball, just nicking it with the tip of his glove so that it looped skyward, toward the outfield, a total disaster.

Josh's brain told him it was over. The runner would never trip twice, and he didn't. Still, it wasn't over. Zamboni had done the right thing, too, and it was Zamboni, backing up Josh, who snagged the ball. If Zamboni had tried to make the throw home, it would never have happened. But he didn't.

Zamboni tossed the ball to Josh, underhand like a relay so Josh could barehand the ball, crank his hips, and fire it to home plate. Josh did just that, sending a rocket to home, pinpointing the catcher's mitt so that the ball arrived at the perfect spot just as the runner slid. A cloud of dirt filled the air. The umpire leaned into it, his face disappearing in the dust. Everyone in the stadium held a breath.

CHAPTER FIFTY-TWO

THE UMPIRE STRAIGHTENED HIS back, his arms extended in front of him as though he still hadn't made up his mind about the call.

"Out!" he suddenly bellowed, his thumb flying back up over his head with the signal.

Josh jumped four feet in the air with a whoop. Zamboni jumped on him from behind, tackling him in the grass, laughing and screaming that Josh was the greatest ever. Together they laughed, got up, and ran for the swarm of teammates in a pile over the top of their catcher. The Lyncourt All-Stars were going to the Little League World Series, one of only eight teams in the entire country, and one of only sixteen in the whole world.

Finally the team got to its feet and shook hands with

their opponents, then milled about their dugout, accepting congratulations from parents and friends. Josh's sudden loneliness cut through the spell of the big win. Zamboni accepted an enormous hug from Diane, and the pang of envy made Josh turn away. It was the first time in his life that his parents—at least one of them—hadn't been at a major event. Not even Jaden had been able to make the trip.

Josh stuffed equipment into his bat bag, then helped Coach Q pick up the team gear and load it into the big bag, trying to ignore all the hugging, kissing, picture taking, and backslapping going on around him. On the bus ride home, the camaraderie of his teammates brought back some of the thrill, but even as they sang "Pants on the Ground" as they pulled up into the parking lot at Grant Middle School and Benji planted a big kiss on his cheek, Josh couldn't help feeling hurt at the missing piece of his puzzle. The sun had gone down long ago, but the darkness only added more thrill to the parking lot, which glimmered like a carnival. Decorations and balloons fluttered in the night air, and the bugs shot through the cones of light beneath the street lamps like mini-fireworks displays.

When they got down out of the bus, Josh and Benji were greeted by Josh's little sister, along with their moms and dads. Seeing his whole family together in a group gave Josh a rush of hope, but after congratulating Josh, his dad excused himself and pushed through the crowd in the direction of Diane and Zamboni. Josh's mom and Mrs. Lido glared after him, but everyone's attention was diverted when Jaden burst into their midst screaming with delight, clapping her hands and hugging Josh and Benji.

"Now I get to go to Williamsport, too," she said, laughing with joy. "The newspaper is paying for everything, for me *and* my dad. No team from Central New York has ever gone to the Series, and my editor said that the story I did on the regional finals was on a whole new level, thanks to the quotes I got from you guys. I hate to say it, but I never thought you guys could do it, either. Not you and Benji, Josh; I mean with the other guys. I know you could do anything, but the team . . ."

"Believe me," Josh said. "The things that happened were wild. We got lucky."

"Aw," Benji said, "luck is just when preparation meets opportunity."

Josh told them how the last play had ended and how lucky things like that seemed to happen for them several times each game throughout the regional tournament.

"I don't know, Benji," Josh said. "Guys tripping, umps making bad calls that go our way, rain washing out a game we were down by seven runs and the next day their pitcher has bursitis in his elbow? I mean, everything that could have gone right for us did. Everything that could have gone wrong for the teams we played did. I've heard the saying 'I'd rather be lucky than good' before, but I think this proved it."

"You won't be able to count on that in the World Series," Josh's mom said.

"That's what Coach Q said," Josh said, "but you never know, right? I mean, someone has to win that thing."

Josh looked past Jaden, searching the dimly lit faces in the crowd for a sign of his father. He knew from the texts they'd sent back and forth during the week—and from the fact that he saw her at every game cheering for Zamboni like a maniac—that Josh's dad hadn't had a chance to confront Diane yet. Josh figured that now was the moment . . . at least, he hoped it was.

"All the parents brought food and soda," Josh's mom said. "I had a bunch of stuff left over from a wedding we catered this afternoon. I guess everyone wanted to celebrate. There are some chocolate-covered strawberries I know you boys will love, but you better get some before they're gone."

"Is Dad coming back?" Josh asked, still searching the crowd.

"I have no idea what your father will do," his mom said, clearly annoyed.

When Josh spotted his dad, it was over in the shadows where people had parked cars by the grass to make room for the party. He stood in front of Diane's Audi, gesturing at her with his hands while Zamboni stood looking with his mouth hanging open. Suddenly

Diane—who'd been shaking her head—burst into tears. She pointed to Zamboni and he got into the car.

Josh's dad looked like he was still yelling at Diane when he brought his face close to hers and she slapped him hard enough to jar his head sideways.

Diane then jumped into the Audi and raced off with a yip of her tires when she hit the street. Without bothering to see if anyone else had witnessed the fight, Josh started toward his father, calling out to him.

If Josh's dad heard him, it made no difference.

His dad got into the new Camaro and took off in the direction Diane had already disappeared. Josh could only stand and watch until the last red flash was swallowed up by the night.

CHAPTER FIFTY-THREE

JOSH LAY IN BED staring at the slanted ceiling close enough to his face that he reached out and ran a finger along a crack in its sandy surface. His stomach clenched and twisted, and sleep danced like a tiny figure in the distance of his mind, miles away. He rolled on his side and took his phone from the nightstand, cracking it open so that blue light filled the small space of covers, pillows, and slanted ceiling.

No messages.

Josh dialed his father's phone again, getting voice mail right away. He snapped the phone shut and lay back again, trying to recall if he had ever felt this helpless before at any time in his life.

The hope that his father would soon be home and life back to normal had grown so large that it crowded his brain and, still, something smelled wrong. How could his father have chased after Diane when she hit him like that? How could he not have ended it by now? None of it made sense to Josh, and the fact that it didn't make sense scared him, because he knew that in the world adults called their own, sometimes insanity ruled.

At the sound of a car coming down the street, Josh grabbed his covers. The low, smooth rumble got closer. Josh bolted up from his bed, banging his head on the ceiling. He didn't care. He scrambled to the window, threw it open, and slipped out onto the roof. His toes curled, bare feet clinging to the rough surface of the tar-paper shingles, and his hands gripped the corner of the house so he could peer around front, down the driveway, and into the street.

What he saw almost made him fall. Then he wanted to jump.

Resting at the bottom of his driveway was the red Camaro. The driver's side door opened, and Josh saw the enormous shadow of his father get out. But when the car's inside light went on, Josh could also clearly see, sitting in the passenger seat and looking into the mirror like she belonged there, Diane Cross.

CHAPTER FIFTY-FOUR

JOSH'S HANDS SLIPPED FROM the corner of the house and he waved his arms to keep his balance. When he found it, he froze, unable to move. His bare feet clung to the roof and he stood half crouched like the survivor of some terrible shipwreck. As his father's giant figure strode up the driveway, Josh could only stare. When his father reached the side door at the kitchen beneath Josh, he stopped and looked up with his face awash in the glow of the streetlight from two doors down.

"Josh?" his father said. "What in the world are you doing up there?"

His father's voice carried with it more than a hint of anger.

"I'll get down," Josh said.

"No," his father said, "you can stay right there. I don't

need you messing around any more than you already have."

"I've been trying to call you," Josh said.

"My phone is off," his father said. "I needed you to hear this face-to-face, Josh. Man-to-man. What you did? I guess a part of me understands it, but I'm so disappointed. That's not even the right word. I'm disgusted at what you did."

Josh felt one foot slipping. He lost his balance and thought he'd fall for certain. That frightened him more because he thought his father wouldn't even try to catch him than because of what the fall would do.

His hands grasped desperately at the side of the house and found a cable TV wire. Instead of falling to the blacktop, Josh grabbed hold of the cable and turned in midair, his knees scraping the tar-paper shingles before he righted himself on his hands and knees, clinging to the roof now like a cat.

"Get back inside," his father said. "I don't want you breaking your neck."

"Why does that even matter to you," Josh said, spitting the words out with as much poison as he could muster.

"You're still my son, Josh," his father said, almost weary now. "I still love you, but telling lies about people, trying to make them look bad, that's one of the worst things you can do. That's no way to go through life, and you have to know that. I have to teach you, whether I live here or not. I'm still your father."

"What lies are you talking about?" Josh asked, his voice rising.

His father huffed and folded his arms across his chest.

"You know," his father said in an annoyed tone. "Don't make it worse by pretending."

"I have no idea what you're talking about," Josh said, wrinkling his forehead.

"Diane," his father said, gritting his teeth in anger. "She met her ex-husband because they're working out a custody situation for Marcus. She's trying to keep him in that private school, and it costs money. She's not *seeing* her ex. That . . . that kiss? Please, Josh. That was nothing. That's how you'd kiss Gran. Diane is doing everything she can to take care of Marcus, and no one can blame her for that. That's not her betraying me. The only one who did that was you."

"Dad . . ." Josh said, the words clogging up his throat like Kleenex in a drain.

"Dad, yes," said his father. "But does that mean I have to live according to whatever you want? You think it doesn't matter what's going on in my life? Is it really all about you?"

"It's not," Josh said, his hands groping the rough shingles to keep from slipping off the edge.

"You're right," his dad said. "It's not. I've found someone who makes me happy and you want to destroy it? You've got to grow up, Josh. You can't just get everything you want."

Josh couldn't even speak.

"Part of me doing what I have to do is coaching the Titans," his dad said, "and we've got a tournament in Philadelphia. Another part of me thinks we need to get a little distance, have a cooling-off period. What I'm getting at is that I'm not going to be able to make the Little League World Series."

Josh felt a chill. He stared at his father's dark, empty eyes and moved his head slowly from side to side instead of saying the word *no.*

"Dad!" Josh leaned forward, urging the sound of his voice to break through the shell of his father's heart, but his dad was already gone.

CHAPTER FIFTY-FIVE

WHEN JOSH OPENED HIS eyes, his mind whirled, remembering the night before and the angry words. He bolted upright, choked by panic, digging into the covers like a dog might go after a bone in a flower bed. He found his own legs and pressed his fingers into their muted flesh, still feeling nothing. A groan spilled from his lips. He swung his body sideways, stumbling as he left the bed.

The burning needles he felt in his feet when he hit the floor added to the panic. He slapped at his legs as the burning grew, then realized they had only fallen asleep because of the twisted position in which he'd slept. Josh breathed deep and then began to laugh out loud.

A soft knock sounded at the door and his mother said, "Josh? Come on. I thought you were desperate to do this thing. The Lidos are out front."

Josh thought about his father again, and the wound in his heart opened, flooding him with sickness. To play in the World Series without his father watching—no, with his father intentionally *not* watching—made it seem almost pointless.

But as he pulled on his clothes, the thought of getting out onto those fields and just playing baseball against the best of the best from all over the world sparked his spirits again. He jogged down the stairs and downed a glass of juice before accepting a banana from his mom for something to eat on the ride.

"Take that bag, too," his mom said, pointing to the countertop. "I made some sandwiches for the bus trip. Enough for you and Benji both. You need to eat to win."

"Thanks, Mom," Josh said, kissing and hugging first his mom, then his little sister and grandmother before shooting out the kitchen door and climbing into Mr. Lido's pickup truck.

When they arrived at the school parking lot, Mr. Lido told them he'd be down the next day right after work to catch their first game.

"Will you make it in time?" Benji asked.

"Don't worry," Mr. Lido said, "I'm leaving work early. You think I'm crazy? What kind of dad would miss his kid playing in the World Series?"

"Just my dad," Josh said, the words spilling from his mouth.

Mr. Lido gave Josh a questioning look and asked, "Really?"

"Really," Josh said.

Mr. Lido's face turned red. "Well, I didn't mean it like that. I'm sure your dad has things he's got to do, Josh."

"That's okay, Mr. Lido," Josh said. "I know what you mean. Thanks for the ride."

They got out, waved good-bye, and closed the passenger side door.

"Don't worry about him," Benji said as they climbed the steps to the waiting bus. "He talks too much. That's part of the reason he and my mom aren't together. That's what she says, at least."

Josh was too embarrassed about the whole thing with his father to even want to discuss it with Benji, so he didn't. However, during the trip, he texted back and forth with Jaden, explaining to her what had happened and bemoaning that the situation looked hopeless, all the while keeping up a cool appearance with Benji.

The two of them settled into their seats and plugged headsets into Benji's compact DVD player to watch a copy of Benji's favorite baseball movie, *The Natural.*

Right before it ended, Jaden texted that Josh should contact his dad, text him, tell him how he felt, and let him know how much it would mean if he could come to even one game of the Series. Josh didn't respond. He let the movie play out, enjoying with Benji when Roy

Hobbs hit a ball so far and hard that it blew up the stadium lights. He and Benji smiled at each other.

"You could do that someday, I swear," Benji said.

Josh felt his face warm and he offered Benji one of the sandwiches his mom made. When they finished eating, Benji put his head against the window and began to snooze. Josh took his phone out and, after half an hour of careful thought and writing and rewriting, he had a text to send to his father.

dad. i no ur mad but i luv u n only want us 2 b togthr. im so sorry 4 what i did n that u feel bad. i wld do anything 2 hv u c me play in w series. pls pls come

After that Josh stared out the window at the passing mountains and trees until Benji woke and the bus pulled into Williamsport, where banners hung across the street to greet the best Little League teams from around the world. The sidewalks downtown teemed with people packed together like schools of fish. The blue sky above was painted with streaks of white clouds.

The bus carried them across the river and out to the International Complex, where the Little League Museum rested at the bottom of a hill. Above that the dormitories stood overlooking the field, the town, and the mountains in the distance. As Josh and his teammates got off the bus, a pleasant breeze brought the scent of fresh-cut grass, drawing them to the crest of the hill. Below, the V-shaped stadium stood empty and massive, patiently awaiting the forty thousand fans who would pack its seats and the surrounding hillside only nine days from now.

The dream of making it that far, to the championship, bounced around the inside of Josh's head like a Super Ball gone crazy. Six games, that's all they had to win to be the world champions.

Six games!

The team got moved into their dorm rooms before orientation. Then they went to a picnic where the players not just from the eight U.S. regions but from all over the world—this year Japan, Mexico, China, Brazil, Saudi Arabia, Germany, Canada, and the Dominican Republic—got to mix and talk and exchange stories. After the picnic, buses took them to a place outside the town where eight enormous trucks waited to pull trailers that each held two entire teams as they went through the center of town in the middle of a giant parade. People lined the streets cheering for them, and the players waved back with giant grins.

That night Josh and his teammates had chicken pot pies for dinner in the dining hall, then went swimming and milled about the activity center before having ice-cream sundaes and finally dropping off to sleep. The next morning the batting coach for the Boston Red Sox put on a hitting clinic, and Josh had to keep Benji—a rabid Red Sox fan—from marching right up to the man in the middle of his presentation to get a cap autographed. The excitement of the experience had steadily washed away the funk Josh felt over his father and family situation back home. But after the opening ceremonies and the team picture on the hill overlooking the stadium, when Benji's mom and dad pulled him off to the side for a family photo of their own, Josh felt a stab of regret that his mom could only watch on TV and that his dad might not watch at all. He thought about the text and wondered if his dad would even read it.

Josh looked around and noticed that Zamboni was doing the same kind of family photo. He knew Zamboni must be excited to have Right Cross there along with Diane, but he couldn't help wondering if his own father knew about it, especially when Right Cross slipped his arm around Diane's waist and pulled her close even after the picture had been taken. When they finished with their photo, Josh saw Diane separate from Right and Zamboni and move his way. He averted his eyes and began to shuffle off.

He didn't get far before Diane's voice rose above the rest, calling his name out clearly.

Josh could only stop and turn.

"Josh," she said, sounding hurt, "can I speak with you?"

Josh said nothing. Diane leaned close and her voice turned cold.

"Spying on me and showing your father that video wasn't right," she said, her eyes locking onto his. "Your father and I share something special. I know you may not like it, but I'm a part of his life and he's a part of mine."

Rage boiled up inside of Josh. He tried to contain it as he said, "I'm not the one who kissed *him,* you are." Josh pointed at Zamboni's father.

Diane looked around and lowered her voice. "What I do or don't do with my ex-husband has nothing to do with you."

"It has something to do with my dad," Josh said.

"Well," Diane said, forcing a smile. "Marcus's father will be here all week, and your father already knows he's here because I told him. It may not make sense to you, but honestly? This is about Marcus. He's dreamed of this for years, and he wants his father here to see him."

"I want my father here, too," Josh said.

Diane puckered her lips and said, "Well, that's between you two. But I think how I get along with Marcus's father is my own business, and the best thing for everyone is for you to mind yours, don't you think, Josh?"

Josh could only stare with his mouth hanging open.

Diane stepped back, smiling and sweet now, and said, “So, we’ll be seeing you around, Josh. Good luck in the game.”

Josh stared hatefully at her as she walked away.

It was at that moment that someone tapped Josh on the shoulder.

He turned around, shocked to see who it was.

CHAPTER FIFTY-SIX

"I THOUGHT YOU WEREN'T going to be here until tomorrow," Josh said. The Lyncourt team didn't play its first game until the next afternoon.

Jaden shrugged and grinned. "My dad was able to switch schedules with another doctor. He just dropped me off and went to check us into our motel. I begged him to come down early so I could spend some time with you guys before you got too distracted with the tournament."

Josh gave her a funny look and asked, "Really?"

Jaden looked around, then lowered her voice and said, "That's what I told him, but the real reason is *them*."

Josh looked back over his shoulder at Zamboni and his parents.

"What about them?" he asked.

"After we texted yesterday," she said, "I had a hunch. I rode my bike over to where she lives and I saw them together again. They were packing her car for the trip, and they got in and took off, together! He left his car on the street just down from her house."

Josh waved her away with his hand, shaking his head. "It won't work, Jaden. He doesn't want to hear it. I told you that. My father is crazy mad. Showing him that picture ended up making them closer than they were before."

"That's because she's an expert liar," Jaden said, narrowing her eyes. "But we've got the truth on our side."

"It hasn't helped so far."

Jaden shook her head. "Don't be that way. The truth always wins out. We just have to show him."

"I just don't know how, Jaden." Josh let his head drop. "Part of me doesn't even want to think about it."

"You can't just give up," she said.

"Okay," Josh said, "let's say I don't give up. What are we going to do?"

Jaden leaned even closer to him and said, "Just listen."

CHAPTER FIFTY-SEVEN

"IF I'M RIGHT, ZAMBONI'S dad didn't make this trip just to watch baseball," Jaden said. "You haven't seen him at any of the other games, right?"

"This is the World Series," Josh said.

"Right," she said, "but it's also just down the road from Towanda."

"What's Towanda?"

"Remember that gas lease business that went bankrupt?"

"Sure."

"Their partner was from Towanda," she said. "I checked him out, too—Andre DuBois. He actually went to jail back in the mid-nineties. I bet they're going to meet with him while they're here. You said your dad was supposed to cough up some money for them, and

I'm betting the deal goes down right over there."

Jaden pointed off away to the west.

"They're staying at the Quality Inn Motel," she said.

"How do you know that?" Josh asked.

Jaden shrugged. "I called all over, pretending to be her and saying I wanted to confirm our reservation. Only took me five tries."

"What good does it do, though?" Josh asked.

"Now we know where they're staying," Jaden said, "I've got a way we can listen in on what they're saying."

"What who's saying?" Zamboni asked, walking up on them suddenly.

CHAPTER FIFTY-EIGHT

JADEN LOOKED PAST ZAMBONI and Josh turned as well to see Right and Diane walking away.

"You'd like to see your parents back together, right?" Josh asked.

Zamboni clamped his mouth shut and nodded.

"Me too," Josh said. "But neither of us is going to see that happen until my dad and your mom break up. Jaden has a plan."

"There's a guy named Andre Dubois," Jaden said. "Ever heard of him?"

Zamboni shook his head.

"Here's his picture," Jaden said, removing it from her shoulder bag along with a mini–tape recorder.

"How's a meeting with him gonna break up my mom and his dad?" Zamboni asked.

Josh thought quick and said, "They're doing a business deal together. My dad is getting the bank to loan them the money. This Dubois guy has been to jail more than once. If my dad knows they're meeting with him or doing a deal with him, he's going to go crazy."

"There's nothing wrong with risky deals," Zamboni said, scowling. "That's how you make it big."

"That's true. But my dad? Well, he wouldn't buy a lottery ticket if it was half price. He hates gambling or anything risky at all. He'll go ballistic, and that's what we need, right?"

"Ballistic over a business deal?" Zamboni said.

"Trust me," Josh said. "He's putting everything on the line—his Nike coaching contract. He's going to go nuts if he thinks there's a chance of losing it."

Josh could almost see the wheels turning in Zamboni's head.

"Okay," Zamboni finally said, "maybe it can work."

"So," Jaden said, glancing in the direction Zamboni's parents had gone, "you'll help us?"

"What do I have to do?" Zamboni asked.

"Quick," Jaden said, taking out her phone and punching some buttons before handing it to Zamboni, "catch up to your parents and see if you can slip this into that big purse your mom carries."

"What?" Zamboni said, taking the phone.

Josh's phone rang and he saw that Jaden had dialed him. He looked at her in wonder. She took his phone and answered the call; then, to Zamboni, she said, "You've got to hurry. Trust me, this will work. Just do it."

Zamboni gave her a doubtful look but turned and jogged off after his parents.

CHAPTER FIFTY-NINE

LATER THAT NIGHT, OUTSIDE the dormitory, beneath a streetlight that held back the darkness, Josh stood with Jaden and Zamboni. Not only had Zamboni successfully planted Josh's cell phone in his mother's big red purse with the speaker phone on, he also learned that his parents were to meet Andre Dubois for a dinner in town. The red light on Jaden's cell phone glowed, and they could clearly hear the sound of Diane and Right Cross along with Andre Dubois at that dinner.

But after listening in on their conversation for nearly fifteen minutes, Josh began to think that Jaden had been wrong.

Josh opened his mouth to ask, "What if—"

"Shhh," Jaden said, cutting him off. "Listen. They just said something about money."

"I told you the contract is signed and sealed. It's all set," Right said. "You just give me the money and that contract is all yours."

"Where's the contract?" Dubois asked.

"In my hotel room," Right said. "Nice and safe."

After a minute of silence, Dubois said, "How'd you get him to sign that thing, anyway?"

"Why wouldn't he?" Diane asked.

"Obviously he trusts you," Dubois said.

"That's what Diane does best," Right Cross said. "She earns people's trust, shows them how everyone can win. Hey? What's the matter, sweet cake?"

"Nothing," Diane said.

A moment of silence followed, broken only when Dubois lowered his voice and said, "Not everyone's going to win in this, you know, Right? What's going to happen when this chump finds out his money is gone?"

"What?" Right Cross said with sarcasm. "He'll have all these leases, and who knows? He might discover some gas after all."

The two men had a laugh together.

Dubois said, in a nasty voice, "There'll be plenty of gas, all right . . . if he eats enough baked beans."

The two men laughed even harder.

Then the waitress came and brought their check.

After a moment of silence, Diane said, "I . . . I don't feel very good. Excuse me a minute, will you? I'll be right back."

Diane's chair scraped and her heels clicked as she walked away.

Josh couldn't help looking at Zamboni. Even in the glow from the streetlights, Josh could see he had turned red. Zamboni hung his head so that his long hair shielded his face.

"And you wonder why I'm a loser," Zamboni said in a mutter. "She's a chump and he's crazy."

"You're not a loser because of your parents," Jaden said. "You're a separate person, Z. You can be better."

"But I'm not," Zamboni said, and when he raised his head, welled-up tears glistened in his eyes. "I'm the jerk."

"You're a good baseball player," Josh said, putting a hand on his back.

"Not really," Zamboni said. "Not compared to you."

"Think about those plays you made at the regionals," Josh said. "You don't catch that pop fly or make that underhand toss to me and we wouldn't even be here."

"You can change anytime you want," Jaden said. "It happens. Sometimes people just decide, and that's it. They just start doing the right thing."

"It's too late," Zamboni said. "They already did what they did. They got his dad's money."

"Not necessarily," Jaden said. "It might not be too late."

"But he signed the deal," Zamboni said. "You heard them."

"He signed it, but money from a bank doesn't get transferred on a weekend." Jaden waved her hands in the air. "We can stop them."

"My dad won't listen," Josh said. "She'll tell him they're talking about someone else. I can't beat her at that game."

"You're right," Jaden said. "That wouldn't be enough."

"What else is there?" Josh asked.

"The contract," Jaden said. "It'll prove they signed the money over to a guy who's already been in jail, a guy no one should trust. Your dad may have trusted Diane, but he's not stupid. He's not going to be okay giving all his money over to a criminal. The tape *and* the contract together? That'll work. I know it will."

"But there's no way to get that contract," Josh said.

"There's always a way," Jaden said, looking at Zamboni.

Zamboni shook his head. "I can't. There's no way I can take something from my dad."

"You don't have to take it," Jaden said. "You just have to get the key to his motel room."

"Who's going to take it then?" Zamboni asked.

Jaden looked at Josh, then said, "We will."

CHAPTER SIXTY

"WE WILL?" JOSH SAID.

"We have to," Jaden said. "It's either that or your dad loses everything. You heard that Dubois guy."

Josh felt anger boiling up inside him.

"You're right," he said.

"It's not like you'll be breaking and entering," Zamboni said. "Here, I've got the key. Take it."

"But wouldn't it be safer just to have you there before they get back?" Jaden said. "I mean, that way, if anything happened . . . They're your parents."

"No way," Zamboni said, shaking his head. "I'm done. I'm going back to the dorm. If something happens and my dad asks me, I have to be able to look him in the eye and tell him I didn't take any contract."

Josh put his hand on Jaden's arm. "Z gave us the

key. I'm the one who should go."

Zamboni flipped open his phone to check the time and said, "You better hurry."

"Why?" Josh asked.

"They already got the check," Zamboni said. "Their dinner is over. They could be back any minute. But maybe you shouldn't try it now. It's nine twenty-seven. We've got curfew at ten."

"I have to," Josh said.

"This is the World Series," Zamboni said. "You miss curfew, you don't play. That's the rule. You can do this tomorrow, or Jaden can do it when we play. You know they won't be in the room then."

"What if your dad gives Dubois that contract?" Josh said. "I'm not leaving until I have it, even if it means I don't play. Nothing's more important to me than this."

Zamboni looked at him for a minute, swatting a mosquito from his face before he said, "Why do you want this so bad? I thought you said you were scared of your dad."

"A little," Josh said, "but this is different. I want him back more than I want the World Series. I don't care. I want him back more than baseball."

Zamboni sighed and looked again at the time. "Okay, but I'm gonna go to the dorm. That's okay, right?"

"I said it was, Z," Josh said. "You did a lot. Thanks."

Zamboni started back up the hill toward the dorm. He stopped and gave Jaden an awkward look before he disappeared into a clump of trees, the glow of his cell phone drifting along like a ghost. Soon the trees swallowed up the soft glow.

"Come on," Josh said.

Jaden followed him past the museum, across the road, through a parking lot, and into the woods. They followed the path, using Jaden's cell phone to help light the way. When they could see the Crosses' motel room, they came to a stop.

They stared at it for a moment before Jaden said, "You should go back, Josh. Don't miss curfew. I can do this."

"No, you can't," Josh said. "I have to. I could never let you."

"It'll be fine," she said. "They're still at dinner."

"I know, but they could be here any second. You should go back to your dad."

"I'm staying with you," she said. "You can't make me go."

"You can stay, Jaden," Josh said, "but you can't go in. I have to do that, and if anyone gets in trouble over this, it will be me, not you."

Jaden didn't move and they stood beside each other, watching together, surrounded by the sound of crickets. Finally Josh stepped out of the woods.

"Okay," he said, "let's do this."

CHAPTER SIXTY-ONE

THEY CAME UP THE walkway and Josh clicked the card key into the lock.

Josh pushed the door open and said, “Don’t come in, Jaden. I mean it.”

The lamp between the two beds had been left on. Josh put his hand on the table beside the window and knocked over a can of hair spray. It clattered into some cologne, shaving cream, and deodorant bottles, spilling them to the floor. Josh picked them up hurriedly and scanned the room, quickly locating Right Cross’s computer and briefcase on the desk. Breathless, and with quavering hands, Josh sprang the latch and popped open the briefcase.

Atop a pile of papers was a manila envelope. Josh quickly examined the top most papers before opening the envelope and drawing free its contents. It was a contract—he knew because it said so—but he didn't know if it was the contract he needed. He flipped to the back page and there it was. In big, bold script, his father's signature.

Josh heard Jaden step into the room and flashed an angry look at her.

"Jaden," he said, his voice hushed but urgent, "I told you not to come in here."

Her face had lost its color, and at first her lips moved without sound.

"Josh," she said, but that was all.

The large, dark shadow of a man appeared in the doorway and growled, "What the heck is going on?"

CHAPTER SIXTY-TWO

RAGE TWISTED RIGHT CROSS'S face.

"Give me that," he shouted, "before I crush you!"

Josh stood hypnotized by the wrinkled red scowl and Right Cross's glittering blue eyes. The contract remained clutched in Josh's hand the way a dog's jaws lock on a bone.

"Hey, Right Cross!" Jaden shouted.

Right Cross turned instinctively.

Jaden snatched up the hair spray from the table, pointed it at Right's face, and sprayed.

Right screamed bloody murder and pawed at his face.

"Josh!" Jaden screamed. "Come on!"

Josh went into action, dodging around Right and taking Jaden's hand as she yanked him out the door and off the walkway, through the bushes, and then across the parking lot for the woods. Josh's lungs burned. His head swam in little stars.

Right bellowed with rage. Josh turned his head to see the crazy ex-hockey player charging toward them, his hands still groping at his own face.

Jaden let out a short scream when she saw him coming. They turned together and sprinted down the path. In an instant it was pitch-black.

Josh felt Jaden's hand snatched away from his own and he heard her scream again.

CHAPTER SIXTY-THREE

JOSH'S FEET TOOK HIM twenty more paces before his brain got him to stop and turn around. Right Cross's angry bellowing echoed through the woods, but even with it, Josh heard a slight whimper. He moved toward it, crouching to find Jaden lying in a tangle.

"My ankle," she said. "I think I broke it."

"Ahhhhhh!" Right Cross screamed, moving closer and closer. "I'll get you! I'll smash you!"

"Put your arm around my neck," Josh whispered.

She did, and he dragged her off the path and into the underbrush behind the thick trunk of a nearby tree.

"Here." Josh eased her into a spot.

Right was almost on top of them now, and Josh and Jaden cowered in their hiding place. They could hear him breathing and the snap of sticks as he approached.

Josh put his head down, resting his forehead in the nest of Jaden's wild hair and feeling the rapid thumping of her heart. Right Cross moved up until he was even with them on the path, then he stopped. Josh could hear heavy breathing, groaning, and growling and imagined Right was still pawing at his eyes.

Then Right began to move again, off down the path in the direction of the dorms, snapping sticks and cursing under his breath, much quieter now, until Josh couldn't hear him anymore above the crickets. They waited, listening, for one minute, then two. Finally, five. It seemed like forever.

"I think he's gone," Josh whispered.

"Do you have it?" Jaden asked.

Josh remembered the contract, clamped in his hand.

"Yes, I do," he said. "Come on."

He helped Jaden up and, with her arm around his neck, they struggled down the path toward the parking lot and the dorms beyond. Soon Josh could see the lights from the street and from the parking lot of the museum, then the dorms up on the hill. Josh felt a laugh bubble up from his throat.

"We made it," he said. "We're out."

"Where do you think he went?" Jaden asked in a whisper.

"Back," Josh said. "Probably took the road."

"He'll be waiting at the dorm," Jaden said. "He's not going to just let you take it."

"No," said Right Cross in a nasty snarl from immediately behind them in the dark, "he's not."

Josh felt Right's hand grip him by the collar and yank hard, throwing him to the ground. Right bent over Josh even as Jaden attacked his back with flying fists. From Josh's hand, Right Cross removed the contract, then straightened to go, shoving Jaden away from him so that she fell beside Josh. Right held the contract up so that the white sheets of paper flapped in the night.

"This is mine!"

Josh looked up at the enraged man as he waved the contract in the air.

A shadow larger than Right grew behind him until even Right sensed it and froze. A massive hand shot out, grabbing Right's wrist and turning it so that he cried out in pain. The pages of the contract fluttered to the ground.

"No," a rumbling voice said, "it's mine."

Josh knew the voice at once.

It was his father's.

CHAPTER SIXTY-FOUR

RIGHT CROSS WOBBLED AND began to sink toward the ground, but he hadn't given up. Aiming for the jaw, he threw his trademark punch. Josh's father smacked it away while his other hand twisted Right's wrist so hard there was a popping sound. Right cried out in pain again, dropping to his knees.

Josh's father twirled Right around, pinning both arms behind his back. He pushed Right's face into the dirt and planted a heavy knee in Right's back, holding him to the ground.

"Get the contract, Josh," his father said. "Jaden, are you okay?"

"I'm okay, Mr. LeBlanc," she said, struggling to her feet. "I thought I broke my ankle, but it's a little better. I just twisted it."

"Good," Josh's dad said. "Josh, grab that contract and get to the parking lot. I'll give Jaden a ride to wherever she's staying after I have a private word with Mr. Cross."

"Are you okay, Dad?" Josh asked, gathering up the contract.

"Oh yeah," his dad said, shoving his knee farther into Right's back so that Right gave a grunt. "I'm just fine. Help Jaden to the parking lot, then run. They told me at the desk that you've got a curfew. Try to make it back there, okay? Here, I've got your phone."

"How?" Josh asked.

"I'll explain later."

Josh took his phone.

9:53.

"I don't think I can," Josh said.

"Get going," his dad said. "I didn't leave my team back in Philadelphia with Coach Moose and drive up here just to see you sit in the stands. Go ahead now."

Josh gave Jaden his arm to help her along. When they reached the parking lot and the comfort of the lights, Jaden said, "Go, Josh. You don't have much time. Don't be late. If you run, you can make it."

Josh looked at his phone again.

9:58.

"I don't think I can make it," he said.

"You've got to try," she said, squeezing his hand.

Josh took off like the wind.

CHAPTER SIXTY-FIVE

JOSH FLEW PAST A stream of parents leaving the dorms. Streetlights and car lights were a blur. His legs, lungs, and brain were numb. He weaved and dodged without wasting his breath on apologizing and yanked open the glass door. He dashed across the lobby, heartbroken at the sight of the big clock on the wall.

The minute hand jumped forward.

10:01.

The tournament official sitting at the lobby desk in front of the elevators looked up from his papers and adjusted his glasses. He scowled and looked down at his watch, then up at the clock on the wall. Josh felt his insides melt. He wanted to explain, wanted the official to know everything he'd been through, everything he'd done and why. Then, surely, the official would take pity on him.

The official studied Josh, frowned, and said, "Looked like ten to me when you came through the door, so technically, you're in. Do me a favor, though. Next time? Get back a little earlier. Good luck tomorrow."

Josh grinned and nodded and managed to choke out a "Thank you." He climbed the stairs to his room. Benji gawked at him when he came through the door.

"Dude, did they bounce you?"

"No," Josh said, wiping the sweat from his face and flopping down on his bed. "I made it with about half a second to spare."

Josh then told Benji everything that happened. He texted Jaden to see how she was. She texted him back that his dad was driving her to her motel and would call Josh in a minute.

Josh quickly got ready for bed, then sat waiting, staring at his phone. When his father's number showed up, he answered before it could even ring.

"Dad, you came," Josh said.

"I got your text," his dad said. "I figured I'd surprise you. I was almost here when Diane called and told me about everything that was going on. She had no idea they planned on totally scamming me. She thought she was just helping Zamboni. That's what drives her, not anything bad. Well, when she found out what they were really up to, she warned me right away. When I got there, I saw the mess in Right's room and called Diane. She told me about the path through the woods and I took off after you. Good thing I did."

"Yeah," Josh said, his bubble bursting. "It was."

The silence hung between them for a moment before Josh asked, "What happened with Right Cross?"

"Nothing really," his dad said, his voice tense. "We're all squared away. I don't want to make a big thing out of this. My money's safe, and you're safe, and that's all that matters."

"But she tried to steal from you," Josh said.

"I know," his dad said, "but she thought I'd get the money back, and she did it for her son, Josh. I actually admire that, and, you know, I think sometimes people can change."

Josh had to laugh.

"What's funny?" his father asked.

"That's exactly what Jaden and I said to Zamboni."

"Good," his father said. "Sometimes it's true."

His father wished him luck in the morning and hung up.

Benji grinned at Josh and said, "Good news, right?"

"Not bad," Josh said.

Coach Q came by to tell them lights out.

"Heard you cut the curfew awful close," he said to Josh.

"Sorry, Coach," Josh said, "it was a family thing."

Coach Q frowned. "Well, you can make it up to me tomorrow. Those kids from Southwest look pretty good. Get some sleep."

After the coach turned out the lights and closed the door, Benji asked, "You think we can beat those guys tomorrow?"

Josh thought for a moment, then said, "Anything can happen, right?"

"You don't sound too confident."

"Honestly," Josh said, "everyone on this team has played incredibly well, but we were still lucky just to get here. It sounds easier than it is. Think about it: the best players from all over the world. The best of the best. We'll have to get lucky, Benji. That's my honest answer."

"But we could, right?" Benji said in the dark. "Like *Miracle on Ice*, remember that movie? The USA hockey team beating the Russians? What about a miracle on the diamond?"

CHAPTER SIXTY-SIX

THE DAY BROKE GRAY and gloomy, and maybe that's why the Southwest team, whose home was Arizona, played so poorly. It wasn't that they weren't hitting the ball—they were. It's just that they weren't hitting it well. Their defense was strong. Josh and his teammates—inspired by the ESPN cameras with their glowing red lights—scrambled, scooping up grounders and snatching pop flies like they were a team full of golden gloves. Josh knew, though, that the Southwest squad had powerhouse hitters. He'd seen them in action the day before. They just weren't in sync.

On offense the only thing going for Lyncourt was Josh. The Southwest pitcher burned through the Lyncourt lineup like a blowtorch through a Kleenex. He gave up a handful of walks, but Josh was the lone batter to connect, once putting it over the center-field fence to a rousing applause and the next time grounding out himself. But in the final inning, Josh's earlier home run had been enough to give them a 1–0 lead, and Josh began to believe that Benji's miracle on the diamond might come true.

Josh would only have one more at bat, so devastating was the Southwest pitcher. He looked up into the stands. His father sat there with Diane, giving Josh a thumbs-up and pointing toward the press box, where Josh knew the college and pro scouts sat taking notes on the players of the future. He smiled at his dad, not so much because of the scouts, but just because his dad was there. And even though he wished it were his mom instead of Diane sitting next to him, Josh knew from the previous night and his dad's reaction that Diane wasn't going away. Also, Josh couldn't deny that she'd had a part in saving the day by alerting his father to what had happened.

There were two outs already when Josh stepped to the plate for his last at bat. With a smile on his lips, he eyed the pitcher from Arizona for the third time that day. He could feel the home run coiled up in his muscles, and he ached to deliver it through his bat. The pitcher frowned and wound up, throwing a curveball. Josh read it and let it go by. The second pitch was a slider, and Josh let that pass, too. The third came fast but so low Josh checked his swing. With a 3–0 count,

Josh knew he should let the next ball go too, but the thought of a walk and standing on base to watch the last batter strike out was too much for him.

So he hunted down a low pitch, driving down on it because there was no way he could hit it up and out of the park. The ball hit the dirt halfway to the mound and bounced high, right into the hands of the second baseman. Josh ran for all he was worth, but it was an easy throw to first and he was out.

Josh hung his head, furious with himself and sensing that the pitcher from Arizona had outsmarted him. The pitcher hadn't obviously walked him, but he'd thrown enough junk so that Josh never had a chance to knock it out of the park, and now their 1–0 lead would have to stand if they were to win the world title. Josh jogged to the dugout and got his glove. Coach Q was optimistic, rallying the team with clapping and backslaps.

"We got this! We got this!" Coach Q cheered. "Come on, it's ours. Play D, just play D like you have been."

Josh left the dugout with Callen Fries, who had pitched the entire game. Coach Q stopped the pitcher and said, "Listen, just put them in there on the inside. They'll keep swinging and we'll keep making the plays."

"Okay, Coach," Callen said, heading for the mound.

Josh couldn't argue with the strategy. It had worked so far, so they might as well keep on going with it.

The first batter hit two foul balls before banging

one into the hole between right and center for a single. The next batter popped one up, an easy grab for Josh. The third batter punched a grounder down the first-base line, a fast out, that left the first batter at second. That's when Benji began his chant.

"'Hey batter, batter, batter,'" Benji taunted. "'Swing, batter, batter, batter!'"

Josh motioned for Benji to hold off on his chant, but Benji only stretched both arms wide and bowed. Callen threw his next pitch down the middle. The Southwest batter ripped it. The ball took off for the right-field fence.

Benji backpedaled, shielding his eyes from the sun. The ball began to drop.

Benji reached up, stretching his glove toward heaven.

CHAPTER SIXTY-SEVEN

JOSH WOKE UP IN his own bed, dressed, and stepped softly down the stairs. He slipped through the kitchen and out into the summer dawn. The birds were up, chirruping in their early morning symphony, and from the highway Josh could hear the solitary hum of a passing tractor trailer.

Otherwise, the city seemed to still be asleep.

Josh climbed on his bike and rode to the corner of Wolf Street and Park. He waited only a minute before he saw Jaden pedaling his way, waving like he was some kind of Roman general home from conquering a remote part of the world.

"Hey," he said, back on his bike and falling in beside her.

"Hey," she said back.

They rode down Park Street to the Market Diner, parked their bikes, went inside, and sat down in a window booth. It seemed like everyone who was awake in the city was inside the diner. The current of voices and smells of pancakes and coffee and home fries bubbling in onions swept over them.

"So?" Jaden said. "How are you doing?"

"You mean being a loser?" Josh asked, wrinkling his forehead and hiding behind the menu.

After losing their first game in the World Series, Josh and his teammates never regained momentum. After three losses, they were out of the tournament.

"You sound like Benji," Jaden said. "He's a wreck."

"It's not like he dropped that ball," Josh said. "It went over the wall. There was nothing he could do about it. He knows that. You know I love Benji, but I think he likes the attention. Anyway, we had a great run just to get there."

"Actually, I wasn't talking about baseball," she said, reaching across the table and lowering his menu so that their eyes met. "I meant, how are you doing with your mom and dad?"

"Well," Josh said, "they're supposed to meet for coffee later this week, but that's just about me and Laurel, not them."

"You know they love you," Jaden said, her voice low and urgent. "Them not getting back together has nothing to do with you, Josh."

Josh sighed and shook his head. He raised the menu back up to look at the omelets.

"It doesn't," Jaden said.

They sat for a few minutes with the noisy clatter of plates and silverware and people all around them before Benji and Zamboni arrived. Josh and Jaden slid toward the window to make room and they all exchanged fist bumps.

Benji got right into his menu, but Zamboni sat studying Josh and Jaden

"Don't even tell me you're talking about parents," Zamboni said.

"Sort of," Jaden said.

"There goes my appetite," Zamboni said.

"Mine's already gone," Josh said.

Zamboni looked at his menu and said, "I don't know. Your dad's not so bad. It's no big deal. Let's not even talk about it. We're supposed to be making each other feel good about our tailspin in Williamsport."

Benji made a sound like a dying animal. "Don't mention that place."

"It wasn't that bad," Jaden said.

"Jaden's right," Josh said, setting his menu down on the table before resting his hands in his lap. "We shouldn't be upset about it. We got there, didn't we? How many people do that?"

"Winning isn't everything," Benji said, his face sagging. "It's the only thing."

"Come on, Benji," Josh said. "We had fun, right? I mean, getting there?"

"Some fun, I guess," Benji said, still glum.

"Yeah, when you made that diving catch in Albany?" Josh said, watching Benji brighten before turning to Zamboni. "Or when you gave me that underhand toss and I fired it home to win the regionals?"

Zamboni blushed and smiled, nodding his head.

"Or when I got to write that article about you guys winning that game?" Jaden said, beaming. "My editor said I hit a new level of writing. They weren't even planning on sending me to cover the World Series, but then they did."

"See?" Josh said. "We played against the best that's out there in the whole world, the best of the best. It isn't something we should try to forget. I want to remember how we got there. How we won a lot of games and got better—the whole team. We got to just go out there and play baseball in the Little League World Series. We got to live the dream. And that? Really?

"*That's* the best of the best."

Next from **TIM GREEN!**

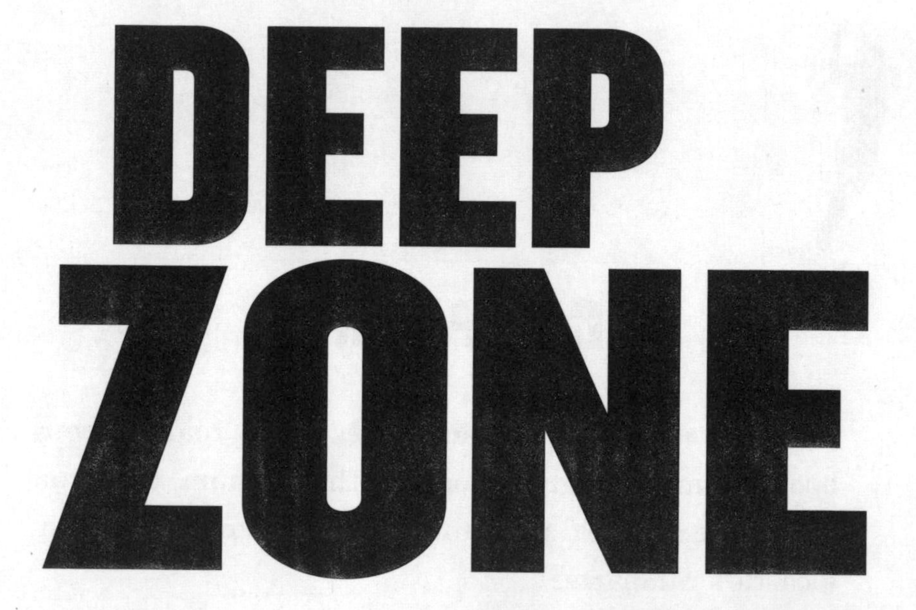

A FOOTBALL GENIUS NOVEL

CHAPTER 1

THE COLD BIT INTO Ty's face. The crowd roared their boos. From the highest point in the stadium, triangular purple and gold pennants snapped like the flags on a castle's ramparts.

"Hey, kid!" someone screamed.

Ty glanced over his shoulder instinctively. A man with a purple construction hat and a stuffed black raven perched on its crown stood at the edge of the railing and shouted until his face went red. "Yeah, you, ball boy! You stink! So do the Jets! Go home!"

The four other men with him wore no shirts, despite the cold. Their bare chests and flabby bellies jiggled beneath purple and black body paint. They hollered their lungs out too, filling the air with puffs of angry smoke. Ty was reminded of the movie *Braveheart,* where half-dressed savage warriors hacked at one another with broad swords. Ty felt like a prisoner, one of the very few people of the seventy thousand packed into the stadium who wore green and white. All else was a roaring sea of purple, black, and gold.

Ty stepped between the benches and the hulking Jets players who sat soaking up the warm air pumped out of the vents beneath their seats. He melted into the safety of still more players, who stood crowding the sideline, their eyes intent on their teammates jogging out to accept the kickoff. Ty searched through the forest of padded legs until he found his brother, tall and lean, built like a greyhound and nearly as fast.

The game would be won or lost in the next few plays, and Ty's brother, the star rookie wide receiver, would likely have a hand in it either way. Thane—or Tiger, as everyone else called him—already had eleven catches and two touchdowns in this nail-biting playoff game. The Baltimore Ravens defense wasn't stupid. They'd be ready for Thane on this final drive, knowing that taking him out of the game would do more than anything else to keep their 27–21 lead.

Ty's older brother looked down, put a hand on Ty's shoulder, and gave him a wink.

"You worried?" Ty asked.

His brother looked across the field at the Ravens bench and the defensive players strapping on their helmets and slapping each others' shoulder pads.

"Just their deep zone," Thane said. "That's all."

"Deep zone?" Ty asked.

"No matter how hard you run, if they're in a deep zone, they're already back there waiting for you." Thane put his own helmet on and snapped up the chin strap. "It's a good way to take away someone with speed."

"That's you," Ty said.

"You and me both. Fast like Mom." Thane smiled, but Ty frowned. Yes, Ty played the game, too, the same position as his older brother, and he was fast, and their mom had been a sprinter in college. But their mom died more than a year ago along with their dad in a car crash, and Ty didn't like to talk about his parents. It especially bothered him when Thane talked like they weren't gone.

They were gone. Nothing could change that.

The whistle blew. Players on the kickoff team streaked past. Helmets popped and pads crunched. Players grunted and roared. Another whistle, and the Jets offense—including Thane—ran out onto the field to begin their final drive.